A Further Twist of Lyme

~

David Ruffle

Paperback ISBN 978-1-78092-717-6
ePub ISBN 978-1-78092-718-3
PDF ISBN 978-1-78092-719-0

Published in the UK by MX Publishing
335 Princess Park Manor, Royal Drive, London, N11 3GX
www.mxpublishing.com

Cover layout and construction by
www.staunch.com

It is no small thing

To have enjoyed the sun

To have lived light in the spring

To have loved, to have thought, to have done.

-Matthew Arnold, Empedocles on Etna

The past is but the beginning of beginning

and all that there is and has been

is but the twilight of the dawn.

-HG Wells, The Discovery of the Future

Also by David Ruffle

Sherlock Holmes and the Lyme Regis Horror

Sherlock Holmes and the Lyme Regis Horror (expanded 2nd Edition)

Sherlock Holmes and the Lyme Regis Legacy

Holmes and Watson: End Peace

Sherlock Holmes and the Lyme Regis Trials

The Abyss (A Journey with Jack the Ripper)

A Twist of Lyme

Sherlock Holmes: The Lyme Regis Trilogy (Illustrated Omnibus Edition)

Another Twist of Lyme

For Children

Sherlock Holmes and the Missing Snowman (illustrated by Rikey Austin)

As editor and contributor

Tales from the Stranger's Room (Vol.1)

Tales from the Stranger's Room (Vol. 2)

For Kath, Liz, Reg, Mick and Andrew

Meet the Hamiltons…..yet again.

Michael Hamilton 59 Reviewer, although not for much longer. Husband of below.

Judy Hamilton 57 Writer, although not for much longer. Wife of above. Mother of below.

Katy Hamilton 26 Performer. Daughter of above. Sister of below.

Annabelle Hamilton 23 Undecided graduate, although not for much longer. Sister of above.

Formerly living: Greater London.

Now living: Lyme Regis, most of them, although not for much longer.

Read on to learn even more…as we move been present day, the recent past and the future.

Chapter One

Michael Hamilton was torn and somewhat indecisive, but everyone knew that. He was like that regarding everything. Exercising his mind today was the question whether to have a birthday party or not. On one hand, he had nearly reached the age of sixty, a cause for celebration surely. Then again, on the other hand, he had nearly reached the age of sixty and there were such things as slippery slopes, something he knew all about. Would it be all downhill from here? Was there any reason to celebrate? Should he hold a wake?

Fortunately, it was out of his hands as Judy, his wife of thirty-two years was making the decision for him. Michael didn't always find decision making easy. Never had. Most likely never will. The only fly in the celebratory ointment was that on this occasion at least, Judy seemed quite incapable of making up her mind either. She had been pleasing Michael for all of those thirty-two years plus a few months prior to their marriage where she had been equally pleasing towards him. Yet she still, on this occasion at least, could not always gauge Michael's reaction to surprises, for she had long ago decided that if she were to go down the big birthday bash route then it would have to be the surprise route, the mystery tour as it were. And Michael had never found handling surprises easy.

Michael had sounded Judy out on the subject of a party. She had been non-committal.

Judy had sounded Michael out on the subject of a birthday party. He had been non-committal. Both pressed on with their plans such as they were or not as the case may be.

Life in Lyme for them had changed very little over the years even allowing for Katy and Annabelle growing up. Rather too quickly in Michael and Judy's eyes, particularly Michael's, with the girls themselves having a somewhat contrary view. Katy was now twenty-six and currently touring in a revived, re-worked and re-imagined production of Sandy Wilson's 'The Boyfriend'. Katy was playing the part of Polly Browne and in a change, (well, it is re-imagined) instead of falling for young Tony Brockenhurst, she forms an attachment to Madame Dubonnet. And Hortense. Ooh la la indeed. Fair enough, it wasn't the West End, but the Theatre Royal (which had never been graced by Royalty) in Throdnall had attractions of its own allegedly although no one was too sure what they were, likewise Throdnall itself.

Annabelle had sailed through university, had worked hard and played hard and had even exited with a degree or two and had also left behind a broken heart or two. She was balanced like that. And now, she was taking a year out to 'find herself' as she put it and decide what direction she wanted to go in. For now, it was a southerly direction as she had announced to her mum and dad that she would best be able to find herself in Australia. Michael and Judy had suggested various alternatives, but none met with Annabelle's approval. Australia it would be. Possibly.

Michael who compared with so many things in his life, had always found reviewing easy, now found that he was no longer so enamoured of that life. He felt and rightly so that he had given his best years, such as they had been, to the world of theatre, music, restaurants, galleries and pig farms and now as he entered his perceived twilight years he had decided that retirement was looking a highly admirable state to be in. Not that he wanted to come to a full stop; he had irons in the fire, fingers in pies. Not literally, that would be hideous. He had recently entered the world of local politics or to be strictly accurate, he had not entered it, but more of that later.

Judy was also contemplating a full and complete retirement. She had been producing novels involving government operative (spy to you and me) and tennis star, Bradley Steel for seventeen years and was feeling as jaded as Bradley's current LTA ranking. In the interest of reality Judy felt that Bradley could not sustain his number one ranking for such an unfeasible length of time and had dropped him to number twelve in the world. Fortunately however, in the interest of national security he remained the highest ranked spy in the world. In fact, as Michael pointed out to Judy, he was only two years short of the national record in that regard, set up by Johnny Stevens. It should be pointed out for those who are not aware of the fact, that Johnny Stevens was entirely and utterly fictitious and had spent forty-seven years residing in Michael's head. Michael had never found disposing of his imaginary friends easy. Johnny Norfolk, star of Barton United and England was still there competing with the master spy for head room.

The sales of Judy's novels had peaked some time before and there had been a falling off in popularity of late. There had been talk of film versions and a mooted TV series, but Connor Milligan, Judy's publisher, had not been able to tie up these deals to everyone's satisfaction. Had Judy grown tired of Bradley Steel? Had she earned enough money? Did she feel that the series had run its course? It was simpler than that; she found it impossible to think up any more plots. Her fans would no doubt cope. Her detractors would no doubt suggest that Judy had only ever used one plot anyway. The current novel therefore, Terror at Roland Garros would be the last in the series and Judy was being tight-lipped about the fate of Bradley Steel. Would she be able to kill him off? Would disposing of him be as difficult for her as Michael disposing of the two Johnnies? Would it be a tennis ball to the temple? Would he become fatally entangled in the net as he strove to make a mockery of his lower ranking? Only Judy knew. Except that she didn't. And even if she did, which she didn't, she would not be telling Michael or Connor at this stage. Which of course she couldn't.

The house was quiet without the girls, (Annabelle being mostly absent and Katy permanently absent) was deemed by friends and what little remained of the family to be too big without the girls, but Michael and Judy had no intention of ever leaving it. A family home does not cease to be a family home because the family has shrunk. Michael knew that to be true, he had read it on a matchbox once.

"Evening, Mike," said Judy, for it was evening.

"Hey Jude, how's the book going?" asked Mike, no longer insanely jealous of Judy's writing abilities. Not insanely no, but maybe a tad.

"It's going well thank you, but I will be glad when it's finished with and I can put my fingers and feet up."

"Definitely going to be the last then?"

"Definitely. Bradley Steel will serve his last serve, lob his last lob and infiltrate his last spy ring."

"Are you going to kill him off? Or let him come out of the closet at last?"

"What?"

"Oh come on, Jude. He has not kissed a woman in the last twelve novels unless you count his mother. And all those meaningful stares across the net meeting his opponent's eyes? Come on, the man is gay!"

"Says the man with two Johnnies in his head!"

"They are strictly segregated, they move in different circles."

"Can you be sure? Perhaps Johnny Stevens has turned up in Johnny Norfolk's dressing room to offer post-match congratulations. Perhaps Johnny is in the bath, Norfolk not Stevens of course. Perhaps Johnny can't help himself, Stevens not Norfolk of course and nature takes its course."

"Nothing like that ever happens in my head, Jude."

"I suspect not, Mike. But remember, your head is not that large to have two red-blooded males sharing it. There must be crossovers you are not aware of. Cross-dressing even!"

"This is all rather silly, Jude."

"Isn't it just? It's like a throwback to the days when we had silly conversations all the time and now we rarely have them at all…any kind of conversation actually."

"Silence speaks volumes sometimes," offered Michael.

There followed a silence which both would have agreed spoke volumes. However it was not a silence which lasted for Irish Meg chose that moment to pop up with a timely and cheery hello.

"Hellooooo folks," she called.

They were never quite sure where to look when they heard Irish Meg for they had never, ever seen her and even her voice had lost some of its clarity and volume not to mention Irishness over the years. To be fair to her, she had been dead for three hundred and eighty nine years and even the most strident vocal cords were bound to suffer over that amount of time.

"Hello, Irish Meg," Judy shouted back. "Any news?"

"None really. That Eddie Fox keeps trying to worm his way back into the captain's favour and gain admittance to our garden. Sorry, folks, your garden, but the captain is having none of it, he is eternally shamed that a member of his family, the pleasantest

11

collection of killers you could ever wish to meet, could have become a balladeer. And do you know what the captain feels is even worse than that?"

"No, what?" asked Michael.

"This Eddie can't even sing, can't hold a note to save his life. Well, when I say his life, I mean...er..."

"We know what you mean," said Michael. Michael and Judy had heard many years ago that Eddie Fox was arguably Hook's finest vocalist. It must be so; the title was official and had been voted for by the readers of the Hook Gazette back in 1967. Admittedly, only thirty-six readers had reckoned entering the poll to be a valid use of their time and out of those thirty-six, only seventeen had actually voted for him, but that was enough for Eddie to top the poll and cement his Hampshire/Surrey position in the pop music world. Eddie duly went on to form The Surrey Seven, noted particularly for their never changing repertoire and quite striking examples of how not to cover well known songs of the day, any day.

"I'll leave you folks in peace," said Irish Meg in a fading voice.

"Regards to the men," added Judy. But all was quiet in the garden. Irish Meg had returned to her life...well you know what I mean.

"Where were we?" asked Michael.

"You were in Bradley's closet, urging him to come out of it, although that of course begs the question just what you were doing in there with him?"

"Hah!"

"You may have a point of course and it would help explain that incident in Omsk."

"My word yes, the Omsk incident, of course."

"You have never found fooling me easy have you, Mike?"

"Meaning?"

"You have no idea what the Omsk incident is have you?"

Michael looked sheepish. It was a skill he had inherited and honed to perfection over the years. "Not really no, well, not to put too fine a point on it, I have no idea at all."

"You did read the book?"

"I have read all your books, Jude. Some of them part of the way through indeed. But you know my memory is not as good as it was."

"So you keep reminding me! It was a memorable scene or so I thought, but it seems not. Even so, I am surprised a scene that involves fourteen bottles of vodka, three pairs of handcuffs, two burly Russian guards, an antique table from Vladivostok, a defecting Russian ballet dancer, a peculiarly shaped vegetable and Bradley Steel in his tennis whites would have passed you by!"

"It does ring a bell actually." Michael noticed the look on Judy's face. Although deciphering looks had never been his thing, he recognised this one. "You made that up didn't you?"

"Most of it, yes," she said, laughing at Michael's discomfort.

"Was there in fact an Omsk incident?"

"Yes, but nothing like that. It was all eyes meeting across a table in a cell and pregnant silences."

"Like that one?" asked Michael after a pregnant silence.

"Precisely!" said Judy after another.

"Although," offered Michael, "that was more of a pregnant pause than a silence I believe."

"I was *expecting* you to say that you know."

"Oh were you? I might have been *anticipating* that from you."

"You think you are *carrying* off this word play now don't you?"

"It's the *family way* we do things around here after all."

"That was awful, Mike. Truly awful, you must be *gest*ating if you think you are going to get away with that. Okay, that was awful too. Let's call it a draw."

"So, what will you do with him?"

"I have no idea at the moment, Mike. The idea of killing him off has its attractions. If I don't I may be persuaded at a later date to bring him back and I really have finished with him. I could just retire him to a cottage in the country, but that sounds so lame. No, I really have no idea. I hesitate to ask it, but do you?"

"Elementary. Have him retire to the Sussex downs and keep bees."

"Thanks, *honey.*"

"The suggestion was short and sweet like me. Didn't want to *drone* on about it."

"Good, that's *nectar* to my ears."

"Well done, you're a fast worker, Jude."

"I am, Mike. *Buzzing* around in my little corner here."

"You are a *hive* of activity all by yourself."

"That's because I am the *queen* of wordplays!"

Michael bowed his head in defeat. He had never taken the time to count how many word plays such as this, they had indulged in over the years and of these how many he had won. A quick (not that quick though) gave him a ball-park figure of 690. Calculating how many he had won was somewhat quicker and easier. It was 23. Although Judy, given the chance to do so, may have disputed that figure. Somewhere in the house a door slammed. Two actually. Annabelle was home. She occasionally returned home. She was good like that.

"Hey, guys. How goes it?"

"We're all right, Annie. I was just trying to beat your mum in a word play."

"Trying would be about right for you, dad. Have you ever beaten mum?"

"Of course, many times."

Judy smiled sweetly and said nothing.

"Yeah, right. Katy says hi, she just sent me a text. Her new show starts in a couple of weeks and she has invited me up to see it. I'll maybe go a few weeks from now; they will be in Banbury then, not so far to go, but far enough."

"What's the show?" asked Judy.

"Sounds odd to me. She said it's *Ophelia Get Your Gun*."

"Sounds…um…interesting," said Mike, "perhaps we'll come with you."

"Or, get this," replied Annabelle, "perhaps you won't and believe me, there is no perhaps about it!"

They did and they didn't.

15

Chapter Two-Politics

A casual vacancy had arisen on the Lyme Regis Town Council. So Michael had read in the local newspaper. And they were often right about these things, the council and the paper.

"Have you seen this, Jude?" asked Michael as casually as he could.

"Yes I have. Surely you aren't…you are, aren't you?"

"I are…am, I mean."

"Why?"

"Why? Do you need to ask why?"

"Yes, as it happens. Why?"

"Well, it would be a chance to give something back to the town. I have time on my hands after all; I may as well use it wisely."

"There's a first time for everything I suppose my political hero!"

"True…er…I think. I'll sound out a few people, kiss a few babies and see what kind of feedback I get."

"Good idea, that gets a *vote* of confidence from me."

"Hah! Who knows, you may *elect* to help me."

"I may just find a *seat* and watch."

"Or a tent from where you can *canvass* opinions?"

"I'll decide thank you, I like to be *independent* about these things."

"As you wish, Jude. I'm quite *liberal* really."

"Don't *labour* the point, Mike."

Another victory for Judy.

In all the years that Michael and Judy had lived in Lyme Regis (19) he or she had never attended a meeting of the council. Remiss of them I know, but there it is. Once Michael had made his mind up to run for council then wild horses would not have kept him away from the next meeting of the full council. Fortuitously, at that time in Lyme there was a definite shortage of wild horses.

The results of Michael asking various folk the question, 'Should I stand for council?' were something like this:

Fourteen people replied with, "Who are you?"

Twenty-one people asked their own questions, all of them uncannily similar, "Were you born in Lyme? Because if not…"

Seven people replied with comments of their own, all of them uncannily similar, "If your family wasn't recorded in the Domesday Book for Lyme, then you have no chance, mate."

On the plus side, five people said they would consider voting for him. All in all, it could have been worse…but not much. Would Johnny Norfolk have been deterred from standing for the committee of the Football Association by a few negative comments? Would Johnny Stevens have been put off by bad vibes from his dream of becoming the controller of MI6? He thought not and nor would he.

Policy. He would need a policy. But what? He had no idea. Who did he think he would appeal to? He didn't know. Michael didn't find decision making easy. Never had. Never will. Maybe he would appeal to the younger generation, admittedly he never had, but as Judy had said, there is a first time for everything. Maybe he would appeal to the older generation who he hoped, with no degree of confidence, would see him as the younger generation. Decisions.

Chapter Three-Decisions

But not Michael's. Judy's. Well, that one decision she still had to make. Kill Bradley Steel off or let him live? Terror At Roland Garros was going really well she felt, everything was gelling nicely. Bradley had advanced to the quarter-finals of the French Open without dropping a set, quite a feat for an older player, let alone one who was also in the throes of bringing down a cartel of arms dealers single-handedly. It was fortunate that the arms dealers were not so active on match days.

It was unfeasible to Judy, to let him go on and win another grand slam title, he had seventeen already which was more than enough, so she had to decide quickly whether his pursuit of the title would end in the quarters and his pursuit of the arms dealers would end in ultimate success or an untimely death. Then, there was the closet question too. Perhaps he and Ross Tallin, his arch tennis-playing foe, should declare their love for one another at the end of a gruelling five setter. Decisions.

Annabelle had a decision to make too, the Australia question, just as pressing as the closet question, not that she knew about the closet question. She was halfway to being certain that she wanted to go down under, but equally halfway to being uncertain. She had always been indecisive, inherited from her father for whom…well we know don't we? She could get a work permit for a year, but what would she do? When she came back, if she went, what would she do then? And the boyfriend question. She had inherited a boyfriend from her university days in Cardiff, who often declared his undying love for him, but often managed to let her down. He made excuses not to come and see her or why she could not come and see him. She suspected the involvement of Bronwyn Davies of Cwmbran who was no better than she should be as someone's mother no doubt said. Bronwyn had made overtures to Ewan before, ironic really, as she played the cello in The Valleys Orchestra. If she wanted to play Ewan too, then she could. He was history. One decision made.

Katy, enjoying her last week in The Boyfriend was contemplating the offer of a date from a member of the audience who had been brave enough to sit through the re-imagining and re-working. Stefan Kowalski, for it was he, seemed struck by her, particularly after she assured him that having the hots for both Madame Dubonnet and Hortense was acting of the highest degree and very much against type. He was suitably assured. She asked Jake Mellor, who was playing Tony Brockenhurst, whether she should accept or not. Jake, who was normally so reliable when it came to giving advice, had no advice to offer on this occasion. Oddly, he seemed to be most put out immensely by the question. Oh well, Katy could quite easily make this decision by herself. Or could she?

Tom Kennedy, Judy's father also had a decision to make. Following the death of Elspeth, his wife, should he downsize? Should he sell the Coburg Terrace home in Sidmouth and buy a smaller property? He was now seventy-nine; did he would to start all over? How long could he keep his independence? Did he even want to carry on this life of his without Elspeth? He had been something big in the city and latterly something big in floristry, but he now found he was not something big in the grief stakes. He simply couldn't handle it. Would he ever?

Fay Kennedy, formerly CEO of Stammersson Inc had now settled into retirement. In her splendid house in Harstad (a parting gift from Stammersson Inc thanking her for all she had done in making Norwegian furniture and accessories such a success) she had no big decisions to make that was true, but was trying to decide when to take the walking trip to Vågsfjorden she had promised herself. There was no hurry, but she had set her heart on it hence the decision making process. She was not to know how momentous this particular decision, when she made it, would turn out to be.

Stefan Kowalski, having taken the bull by the horns and asked Katy Hamilton out was now pondering where to take her. The cinema? A meal? A drive into the Throdnall countryside exploring the scenic highlights? No, that would be far too short a drive. Besides he had no car. Decisions.

Jake Mellor was pondering too. Should he offer Katy advice on this proposed date? Or perhaps more pertinently, certainly to him, should he ask her out himself? Decisions.

Chapter Four-An Ending

The moment could no longer be put off. Procrastination would no longer work. Something must be done...now. Judy was sitting in a part of the loft which manfully doubled as an office. The view was lovely, encompassing the garden and the stream into which no one had tumbled for many a long year. The setting was peaceful, only interrupted now and again by Captain Edward de Vere Fox and his men who occasionally insisted on a bout of swordplay in the garden. In vain did Judy point out that this kind of swordplay was what very possibly got them killed in the first place, but in the Hamilton's garden at least, there was a very fine line between the dead and the living. Still, there was an agreement between the living and dead that the living would...well...go on living and the dead would remain...well...dead, but with free access to the garden to do as they wished within reason.

Mostly, this had worked very well apart from the Eddie Fox incident and the Fay molestation incident when young Thomas could not help himself and touched Fay by the stream. There had been no repeat of the incident.

The day of reckoning, when Bradley Steel's fate would be decided had arrived. Judy, fingers poised over the keys of her laptop, breathed hard and launched into the final few paragraphs in the life of Bradley Steel, spy, tennis player and all-round good guy. They remained poised. Her mind was blank; it had never been so blank. Except it probably had. The fingers twitched once and descended to the keys:

He acknowledged the smattering of applause that accompanied his final walk out of the arena. It was the kind of applause he had heard before, a special kind of applause reserved for champions past their sell by date. It said 'you have been a great champion, we have loved you, we still love you, but it's time to go.' It was time to go; no one knew it more than he. He had spent too many years living on a knife-edge, always looking over his shoulder. He was thirty-six now; he had nothing left to prove in his chosen sport and his chosen profession. He had nothing left to prove to himself. His dual life had eventually drained him, there was nothing left to give, nothing at all.

He had dealt in secrets for as long as he could remember. Secrets shared, secrets betrayed, secrets so hidden they could never come to light, secrets that had spelt life for some and death for others. But now he had a secret of his own. A secret that had to be kept at all costs. He had taken steps, made arrangements that would secure his new life. He had delved into his past, to the training camp at Acton and made contact with...

'Just who would he make contact with?' Judy thought. She had to think of a name and what better name to come up with than Johnny Stevens! She imagined the look on Michael's face when he saw it, he didn't always find surprises easy, but she thought he might just enjoy this one. Should she explain in a footnote where the name came from. She thought better of it. She had always been of the opinion that footnotes play havoc with the rhythm of a story[1].

...his old mentor, Johnny Stevens, well deserving of the epithet living legend. He was renowned in the service for his tradecraft and the tales told about him were many, colourful and maybe even true. He and Bradley had become firm friends and Bradley needed someone he could trust implicitly if his dreams were to come true. A new start, a new identity, which is where Johnny came in...he knew more about this sphere of operation than anyone Bradley knew. He knew that once he took this step he was a marked man. His own service would see him as a traitor or a

---

[1] I concur completely.

defector; he would be forever watching his back. This was something he had become accustomed to; he had been marked out before, but not by his own side. His high profile on the world stage had negated these threats, but all the same he was always on his guard. He would pitch up on a foreign shore, preferably exotic and become the local eccentric Englishman. There was no need of plastic surgery; he knew he could change his features and characteristics without recourse to any kind of enhancement or embellishment. There was a plane waiting at the airport and Johnny Stevens with it. Monies had been transferred into new accounts that no-one would be capable of locating. New identity set up…he was now…

'But who?' thought Judy. Ah yes, in homage once more to Mike, it had to be…

…Jonathan Norfolk, a businessman, an international traveller except he had no plans to travel other than his ultimate destination; the Bahamas.

He stepped out into the Paris sunshine. He didn't see the glint of sunlight that twinkled from the top floor of the building opposite. He didn't hear the crack nor did he feel the bullet that tore into him.

There, she had done it. Bradley Steel was no more. How did Judy feel? Surprisingly good, perhaps she should have done it years before. She suppressed the urge to laugh and then gloriously gave way to it. She felt as free as Bradley Steel although blessedly free of the threat of assassination. Which was good.

24

Chapter Five- Fall and Decline

As local rivalries go, the annual croquet match between Sidmouth WI and their Budleigh Salterton counterparts was as fierce an encounter as any football matches between Manchester United vs Liverpool or Celtic vs Rangers. Sledging, sabotage and dirty tricks were not unknown throughout the history of the fixture, the poisoned Damson jam scandal of 2013 springs to mind, not to mention the roquet/croquet stroke scandal of the previous year when it was felt by all the Sidmouth team that Elizabeth Plunkett of Budleigh was guilty of cheating her way to victory. Sidmouth really needed to win this one. Recent matches had seen Budleigh cock-a-hoop at their overwhelming victories, crowing it seems was very much their style.

Elspeth Kennedy had risen through the ranks to become captain of the Sidmouth team. She was the best woman for the job, everyone said so. Her continuation strokes and triple peels were things of beauty. The lemon drizzle cakes that regularly adorned the tea-table helped cement her position in the team. True, visiting teams did try to bait her with sly references to the almost forgotten, but still infamous Basque Night , but Elspeth was able to rise above all of this, her dignity intact. Indeed, when she thought about that night, which was actually fairly often, she was almost able to laugh. Almost.

The croquet lawn was just a few minutes' walk from the Kennedy's Coburg Terrace home. Elspeth was in an advanced state of nervous tension, so much so she had missed breakfast for only the third time in twenty-seven years. Tom had gallantly offered his assistance in order that the breakfast should not be wasted. He was good like that. The rest of the team members were already assembled, ready and eager, if not especially confident. Losing seventeen matches in a row to your bitter rivals does not go very far in instilling confidence. Self-belief can only count for so much.

Elspeth rallied her team around her in the famous Kennedy huddle. They were urged, cajoled and fired up by a pep talk from Elspeth that rivalled anything Henry V could have come up with for the pre-Agincourt pep talk. For God, Harry and St George is not a patch on for Sidmouth, Elspeth and the WI. The four team members were stirred into what passed for action and scampered on to the lawn in a manner which belied their combined age of two hundred and eighty nine.

After the first three hoop points had gone Budleigh's way, Sidmouth's perennial lack of confidence came back. Cue another Kennedy huddle. Cue some strokes of luck and suddenly Sidmouth were back in the match. Even their opponents' delaying tactics could do nothing to stop their charge. Even the underhand tactic of having Elizabeth Plunkett's husband streak across the lawn could not deter them. 'Seen it all before' was the most quoted remark although not by Miss Catherine Wilcox, who declared that she could not see what all the fuss was about, a little thing like that. Henry Plunkett was considerably chastened. Elizabeth merely nodded.

Sidmouth's spirits rose. Budleigh's spirits plummeted. The game was long over as a contest by the time they came to the final hoop. The Sidmouth team was jubilant. The spectators were jubilant, all seven of them plus a stray dog. Tom, alas, was not there due to an urgent appointment in the Coburg Terrace home with a bottle of shampoo. As the final hoop point was won the Sidmouth team in an outburst of joy and spontaneity high-fived each other. Although due to a lack of mobility from some of them it was more like fairly low high-fives all round.

In the middle of the Kennedy celebratory huddle, Elspeth, almost unseen, slipped down to the manicured lawn. One glance was all it took for her team to recognise that Elspeth had possibly suffered a stroke. An ambulance was called and Tom was fetched.

It was a stroke, the first of a series that Elspeth was to suffer. For the remaining months of her life, speech was limited, movement was limited, but her love for Tom was unlimited as was his for her. He converted the lounge to a bedroom and barely left Elspeth's side for the next few months. Perhaps, he at last proved to be the man that Elspeth always wanted him to be, but frequently wasn't; strong and dependable. The decline was measured in months, but to Tom could be measured in minutes. With each succeeding stroke, less of Elspeth remained; her life was rapidly shrinking and diminishing.

The end came one September morning as the early morning autumn sun peeped through the curtains. Tom said his goodbyes, called their doctor and prepared for life without her.

The funeral was a small affair with family and assorted WI members only. The wreath on the coffin, in a nice touch, was a representation of a lemon drizzle cake and in the spirit of a newly forged friendship, the Budleigh Salterton WI croquet team formed a guard of honour with their mallets raised high as the coffin entered the church. If a funeral can have highlights than that was undoubtedly one. Everyone said so.

Fay stayed on with her father for a couple of weeks to help ease him through the difficult post-funeral period. In spite of his protestations she arranged for a woman to come in daily or when needed to help with the cleaning and cooking. Yes, he was fiercely independent (indeed he had already turned down an offer from Michael and Judy to sell up and move in with them), but she and Judy were happier that someone would be on hand.

The arrangements having been made, Fay flew back out to Norway where her career was winding down (by choice). Early retirement was beckoning seductive fingers in her direction and she had always had a weakness for seductive fingers. Those who knew her best would agree.

Back in Sidmouth, Tom tried to adjust. He would ever after be trying to adjust.

Chapter Six-Ophelia Get Your Gun Time

"So this is Banbury," observed Annabelle both needlessly and accurately as they were sitting outside a High Street coffee shop, sipping lattes.

"This is it Annie, yes," replied Katy. "You sound disappointed."

"No, not really. I don't know what I was expecting really."

"You've been here before anyway, Dad brought us here at least once when we were at Adlestrop for visits."

"Can't remember that at all. Sure I was with you?"

"Where else would you be? And besides it wasn't an easy trip to forget, you managed to vomit in the back, the front and down the side of the car!"

"That was probably Dad's driving did that. How's the new show going then?"

"Ironed out a few problems the first few weeks. It's been a relief to get it up and running. We were rehearsing it by day and performing The Boyfriend at night."

"Talking about boyfriends, how's this Stefan you mentioned? Hot date in Throdnall wasn't it?"

"I don't think there is such a thing as a hot date in Throdnall, but he did his best, poor lamb. He took me to the local social club where he played pool with his mates all night and barely said a word to me other than, 'you okay love?' It wasn't the worst date I have ever been on. Well, actually it was."

Annabelle involuntarily spat out a mouthful of coffee which narrowly missed a Church of England vicar from Brackley who was taking ten minutes out of his day. "Even worse than the date with Zak Curry?"

"Even worse than that yes."

"But Zak took you for a ride on his father's tractor. He got you to help him clean out the chicken coop, tried to get you drunk on scrumpy and managed to spill it all down your dress, which as I recall he gallantly offered to remove. Are you telling me it was worse than that?"

It was precisely what Katy was telling her. Annabelle let out a whistle through her teeth which thoroughly alarmed a nearby Jack Russell which leapt up against the nearest table scattering mugs everywhere. The Reverend Reginald 'Freddie' Raskin, as he mopped his trousers, was now of the opinion that taking ten minutes out of his day had not been the smartest move.

"So no more Stefan. Got your eye on anyone else?"

"I didn't actually say no more Stefan did I?"

` "You're kidding me; you're still seeing him, tell me you're kidding, Katy."

"No kidding! He is here in Banbury at the moment. The second date went better than the first and the third better than the second. I have very high hopes for the fourth."

"Is the fourth…er…when…?"

"More than likely! Mind you, we are in separate hotels. He is staying where you are actually. Anyway, I'm meeting him for lunch, coming?"

"You bet, wouldn't miss it for the world."

Lunch was at the Reindeer, Banbury's oldest inn where, in spite of the local beer being of a particularly fine quality, both Annabelle and Katy opted for beetroot and cabbage cider. The door opened. A tallish guy walked in. Stubble on chin, but otherwise very presentable. Dressed to impress.

"Did you say something, Annie?"

"I may have done. That guy is dressed to impress I was thinking."

"Yes and that's odd, he's never done that before."

"Oh! I see…that's him. He's not bad, Katy, not bad at all."

"Hands off sis, he's mine; I know what you're like. You always fancied my boyfriends."

"Not Zak."

"No, admittedly, not Zak so I suppose we should credit you with some sense."

"That was all a long time ago, I have grown up a bit since those days."

"Yeah, okay. Stefan, hi…this is Annabelle, my sister."

Stefan offered his hand, which Annabelle shook and then wished she hadn't.

"Sorry, sweaty palms. I tend to get nervous on these occasions."

"What, eating lunch?" laughed Annabelle and received a black look from her sister.

"Are you eating with us, Annie? You don't mind if I call you Annie do you?"

Annabelle was momentarily distracted by Katy miming, as only an actress of her standing could, picking up a bag and walking towards the exit while all the time pointing at her with her non-miming arm and hand.

"Yes, that would be very nice, Stefan. Thank you."

Stefan was a mine of information on the play. Unaccountably, he had seen it three times already. His opinion was that Annabelle would enjoy it very much and that a mix of Shakespeare and the Wild West should be on top of everyone's theatre wish lists. As to that, Annabelle would make her own mind up. He told tales of merriment in Gdansk that his father and grandfather had passed down to him. These, understandably, did not detain them for long.

After splitting the bill three ways, they wandered down to the canal side bar which as you may have guessed was situated next to the canal. The bar was an extension of the Mill theatre itself and Katy gave Annabelle a quick tour of the backstage area and dressing rooms. The beetroot and cabbage cider was making its presence known and Annabelle retreated rather sharply towards the toilet she had noticed by the entrance. Rather sharply became much more sharply and before she could gain the haven of the ladies' she managed to clatter into a young man exiting the gents'. He managed a half-smile before his legs folded under him and rather less of a smile as his back came into contact with the hard (very) corridor floor.

Annabelle's bladder dictated there could be no immediate apology; there were priorities here after all. When she came out, shaking her hands (life's too short to use hand-driers) he had vanished. Shame, from what little Annabelle had seen of his stricken face and body he seemed okay. More than okay in fact.

There was a pleasant surprise awaiting her outside. There were Katy and Stefan...and Annabelle's mystery man. 'Well, well,

32

Banbury…things are looking up, thank you very much,' thought Annabelle.

"Annie, this is Jake, Jake Mellor. He is my leading man."

"Actually, Katy, I have already bumped into Jake."

Jake and Annabelle laughed. Katy and Stefan didn't.

"How long are you in town for, Annabelle?"

Nice. He didn't just assume he could call her Annie. She liked that. She liked the fact her pulse was racing and that she was getting rather pleasurably flushed.

"Just tonight and tomorrow. Although…"

"Yes?" queried Jake.

"There's no reason I can't stay a while longer. I mean, there is nothing to rush back for. So, I suppose I could stay on…er…say a day or two, or even three or four…um…"

Katy whispered in Annabelle's direction. It sounded like 'tart', but it could have been something else sounding like tart. Maybe…no, let's be honest, it was tart.

Stefan and Jake were dispatched to the bar.

"Jake's a great guy, Annie, okay?"

"Meaning?"

"Don't mess him around or you'll have me to answer to."

"Older sisters don't scare me anymore. We're adults, we'll do what we like. First you're worried I may have my eyes on Stefan, who to be honest is rather low in the charisma stakes and now you want to keep me away from one of your mates. Chill out, Katy."

33

"I was just saying that's all."

"Okay, you were just saying and now you have said it."

"Everything all right, girls?" asked Stefan, smiling at Annabelle.

"I'm not a bloody girl, Stefan or had you not noticed?"

Jake shook his head and grimaced at Katy.

"Don't shake your bloody head at me, Mellor."

One supposes that neither Stefan nor Jake had ever had the need to negotiate a sibling minefield before. They did not cover themselves in glory on this, their first attempt. They beat a hasty retreat to the sanctuary of the bar.

"Bloody men," exclaimed Katy.

They both laughed. Sibling crisis averted. For now.

Later that evening, a hushed crowd waited expectantly. Although the word crowd is perhaps too strong a word to describe the small gathering in the theatre. Annabelle was sitting next to Stefan who was still waiting expectantly even though he knew precisely what to expect.

When the opening scene began, Annabelle had one of those questions that we all have had at some stage.

"Stefan, who is who here?"

"Shh."

"What?"

"I said shh."

"Yes, I know, but why?"

"Because I'm concentrating and would rather not be bothered by your questions."

'Charming. You're welcome to this one, Katy,' thought Annabelle.

Unexpectedly, during the intermission, Stefan did have the good grace to apologise. Even so, Annabelle thought better of mentioning the other eleven questions she had accumulated during a confusing first act. The second act was only marginally less confusing, which did not inspire too much confidence in the clarity of the third act to come. Still, Katy was acquitting herself well as Ophelia although Annabelle's eyes were drawn to the manly figure of Jake Mellor playing the manly Sheriff Bill Hamlet. He definitely had a certain something that begged to be explored.

Annabelle, deciding she had carried out her sisterly duty, attended no other performance that week, although she did stay on just as she had intimated. Two days stretched to five days. Stefan extended his stay too, Katy appeared to be getting used to having him around. There were five days of leisurely lunches where the four of them chewed the fat, assuming they had fat of course. They occupied themselves in other ways, when not lunching.

After a particularly energetic bout of love-making, exciting, but somewhat perilous in a single bed which struggled to live up to its name, Annabelle rolled over and said (breathlessly), "I can't do this anymore, we have to say something."

Across town, Katy, equally breathlessly, after an equally energetic bout of love-making said, "It's no good, we have to come clean."

"Yes, you're right, Annie," replied Stefan

"I agree, Katy, it's only fair," said Jake.

The next day they all met for lunch at the Barley Mow, a hop, skip and jump out of town. In they came; Annabelle with Stefan and Katy with Jake. Drinks were ordered, menus consulted. Drinks were consumed, food ordered. Food was consumed. The waitress came and went, and came and went again. The conversation was stilted and slow. The waitress was slow, but then again, unknown to our nervous and apprehensive four, she was something of a celebrity. Miss Hannah Tarrant, who at ninety-six was acknowledged as the oldest working waitress in the United Kingdom, possibly the world (there is a dispute still to be resolved which revolves around Eun Kyung in Seoul who claims to be ninety-eight). If this were not claim worthy enough, Miss Tarrant was an international weight-lifter until the age of sixty-five and is still the holder of the Commonwealth senior record of 53kg. She had recently narrowly missed out on winning the British over 90's competition when she fell asleep in the changing room while knitting a cuddly rabbit; she had been knitting such rabbits for fifty-four years, no one knew why.

"Sorry about the chicken nuggets," said the aforementioned Miss Tarrant.

"Sorry, not with you," said a puzzled Jake.

"We have none left. Between you and me, I took them home with me; I am rather partial to them. I hope that clears up the confusion."

They all agreed that had there been any confusion to be cleared up, then the waitress's words would have done the trick admirably, but there hadn't been. Although there was now.

"Thank you," said Jake as he could not of anything else to say.

Katy took a deep breath. "Annie, I have something to tell you."

"I was going to say that too," Annie said.

"What? That I had something to tell you?"

"No, that I have something to tell you too. Shall I go first?"

Katy had no idea what Annabelle was going to tell her, but just to give herself some breathing space and the chance to further compose herself, she agreed that her sister could go first. She nodded.

"There's no easy way to say this, but," Annabelle took a deep breath of her own. "I have been seeing Stefan. Sorry, I know you're going to hate me, but I can't change it."

Katy's reaction was not quite the one that Annabelle had been expecting; she threw her head back and laughed. Laughed so much and so hard that the restaurant's resident first-aider hovered discreetly by the table in case his services were required. They weren't.

"What's so funny?"

"Oh, Annie," Katy replied, wiping her eyes, "My news was that me and Jake are seeing each other as of the last couple of days."

It was Annabelle's turn to laugh, which she did. Jake and Stefan were content to smile rueful smiles. Katy and Annabelle left them to their possible embarrassment and definite rueful smiles and retired to the Ladies for a discussion of a more private nature.

"Katy, you and Stefan…well…"

"Yes, Annie?"

"Well, the fourth date…I mean…did you…er…well, did you?"

"If you mean what I think you mean then the answer is no."

"Phew!"

"You and Jake?"

"No."

"Phew!"

The two phews having solved the matter satisfactorily, they returned to Stefan and Jake, who unbeknown to the girls had been actively involved in a similar discussion although couched in somewhat different terms. The week in Banbury had changed all their lives. Banbury can do that kind of thing. Everyone says so.

OPHELIA GET YOUR GUN

(AKA THERE IS SOMETHING ROTTEN IN THE STATE OF ARIZONA.)

ACT ONE SCENE ONE OUTSIDE THE SALOON BAR. A STAGECOACH IS SETTING DOWN ITS PASSENGERS.

OPHELIA (A GUNSLINGER): Well looky here, I espy a corncracker. Thou shouldst have stayed on yonder farm.

BILL HAMLET: Do you address me fair maiden? Your wit's too hot, it speeds too fast, 'twill tire. (IN AN ASIDE TO FELLOW PASSENGERS): She speaks, yet says nothing. (ADDRESSING OPHELIA): I am no farmer of this I can testify, you are guilty in your haste and ready wit to haze a tenderfoot.

ROSE ENCRANTZ (THE MAYORESS): Ophelia, durst you profess not to know this man. This is the fabled Bill Hamlet, this bold bad man turned good man. Like him that travels, he has returned again. The city's fathers have offered up the post of Sheriff to our friend here.

OPHELIA: He has a villainous low brow. He can be no friend of mine. There is a path of certain enmity between us.

BH: I grieve to hear you say it sweet Ophelia for I look upon your beauty as though I am in the first flush of youth, yes sirree.

OPHELIA: The man is false, he is a lowdown sneaking polecat who is intent on jawin' me to death. Mark my words people the next thing you know he will be comparing me to a summer's day the lickspittle.

BH (IN AN ASIDE): She is a woman, therefore may be woo'd. She is a woman, therefore may be won. (ADDRESSING OPHELIA): That man that hath a tongue, I say, is no man, if with his tongue he cannot win a woman. You are a pretty red heifer and mean as catmeat but I wager I will tame you before the end of summer.

OPHELIA: Methink'st thou art a general offence and every man should beat thee. Thou appeareth nothing to me but a foul and pestilent congregation of vapours. You should be run out of town like the varmint you are.

BH: Yet, spaniel-like, the more she spurns my love,

The more it grows and fawneth on her still. I love you with so much of my heart that none is left to protest. I pledge to thee that before the saguaro has withered and died we will have a hog-killin' time.

OPHELIA TAKES HER SIX-SHOOTER FROM HER HOLSTER AND FIRES A SHOT AT BILL HAMLET'S FEET. SHE WALKS OFF TO ADORING LOOKS FROM THE NEW SHERIFF.

ACT THREE. SCENE FOUR. THE SALOON BAR IN TOMBSTONE

SHERIFF BILL HAMLET ENTERS STAGE LEFT

BH: Alack, I am distll'd almost to jelly with the act of fear. The James gang are without.

ROSE ENCRANTZ : Without what?

BH: The villains are once more abroad. O foul knaves. They seek their bloody revenge upon us.

RE: How so, sweet Sheriff? If they are abroad, how can they thus seek to harm us? Have thou been drinking moonshine again, brave protector of our town?

BH: They are here, their very flesh pollutes the OK Corral. And yet you speak as though you are unsifted in such perilous circumstances. Old man James of evil memory smiles and smiles, the smiling damned villain. That one may smile and smile and still be a villain, what calumny, what falseness and yet I fear it is so in Tombstone. Sweet Ophelia, wouldst thou save us from the very crack of doom which has opened up this very day, this cursed day?

OPHELIA: This cursed day, my lord Sheriff? The James gang are even now bedecked in chains of untold strength in the deepest foulest dungeons of the State penitentiary. Methinks your imaginations are as foul as Vulcan's stithy.

BH: Perhaps I am mad north-northwest, but I have seen what I have seen. Who will grant us deliverance from these men who wouldst treat us most cruelly? Sweet Ophelia, I beseech you once more.

OPHELIA: You, who have played me false these ten years past yet now thou durst seek my benevolence in taking arms against your sea of troubles? My brave Sheriff you must perforce look into your own soul for the deliverance you seek. I will have no part in't.

BH: Methinks the lady doth protest too much. I have a purse here which may yet turn your advantage to our own. Our own fair Rose, Mayoress of our beloved city has given me leave to rouse your spirits with the princely sum of twenty dollars.

RE: I have?

BH: Indeed, sweet lady. What sayest thou, Ophelia?

OPHELIA: Yeomen, bring me my Winchester73 that it may do honourable and bloody business this day.

THEY ALL EXIT STAGE LEFT. THERE ARE SOUNDS OF GUN PLAY AND A CRY OF: 'A HIT, A PALPBALE HIT'.

BOOT HILL CEMETERY LATER THAT DAY

BH: Lay her i' the earth and from her fair and unpolluted flesh may saguaro spring. Yes sirree.

THE REST IS SILENCE.

Chapter Seven-More Politics

The more Michael thought about it, the more he thought he was town councillor material. It mattered not to him (well maybe a little) that the more Judy thought about it the more she thought he wasn't. He attended a couple of meetings of the full town council to get a feel for the way things were conducted. These he expected to be sombre, staid even solemn affairs and other words beginning with S that he could not bring to mind at the time. They were anything but.

The security guards posted at the door were his first clue that his expectations were not to be met in the way he had…well…expected. The second clue was that they were posted inside the chamber.

"Why on earth are security guards needed here?" Michael asked as casually as he could, as casually as anyone could while being frisked from head to toe.

"You'd be surprised, mate," said the tallest and widest of the two.

"I already am."

"Any weapons concealed on you?" asked the marginally less tall and wide one.

"No. No weapons."

"Any sweets?"

"Sweets?"

"Yes, sweets, you know confectionery and the like."

"Yes, I know what you mean, but why do you want to know?"

"If you have any, we may have to confiscate them depending what they are. Marshmallows are fine. Jelly Babies, marginal because they can be used as a missile once the heads have been removed. Mint Humbugs, no chance, they could have someone's eye out."

"Any allergies?"

"Allergies? Why?"

"Just answer the question, sir. Allergies?"

"Country and Western music. And I have no sweets, no weapons, or anything that could be construed as a threat to anyone present."

"Thank you, sir, only we have to be sure after the recent Sherbet Fountain fracas."

"I didn't read anything about that in the local paper."

"It was classified as classified information. The freedom of the press counts for nothing anymore within the Lyme Regis town council, not after the press card fiasco."

"Not a fracas that time?" queried Michael.

"Definitely a fiasco or another word beginning with F I can't quite bring to mind. Please take a seat behind the bullet proof screen and please, sir, no sudden moves."

Michael took his seat behind the bullet proof screen, which to be fair wasn't really bullet-proof, but just a run of the mill perspex screen, and idly wondered if it was there to protect the public or the councillors. The debates that night were all about the finances of the council and how to spend any surplus they may have. Offshore accounts cropped up once or twice. It was agree to spend some extra money on security to aid implementing the latest policy. That latest policy was to ban all teenagers from the town's beaches after 7pm for there had been reports in the local newspapers that young people had been spotted enjoying themselves both on the shingle and the sand. This, the council felt, presented a bad image for the many tourists who were attracted to the town. They further felt that these young people showed an astonishing lack of gratitude for, at huge expense the council had provided two table-tennis tables, three pool tables and a skipping rope. The motion was carried ten votes for with four against.

The debates became more heated as the evening wore on with many an expletive ringing around the chamber. No that expletives particularly bothered Michael, he had after all spent a fair few years travelling to Waterloo on perennially late trains. There were two local reporters present who both had council officers standing by with red pens and they took it upon themselves to periodically erase certain words or phrases that had found their way into the reporter's notebooks. The town council had to remain accountable if only to itself. Michael idly wondered whether the perspex screen was an integral part of the council's transparency policy!

The sentry posts situated on the approaches to Lyme and their continued usage also came under discussion with some thinking the time had come to disband them altogether particularly in view of the falling numbers of tourists who now visited each year. The LYME FULL PLEASE FIND AN ALTERNATIVE RESORT signs had been vandalised so often they were no longer legible. Opinion in the town had always been divided on this thorny issue, but even the hard-liners had mellowed somewhat, after all, the sentry posts were no longer manned by armed guards and the

NO UNDER TWENTIES sign had long since been consigned to history.

The evening, although stormy at times never threatened to become a fracas or fiasco and as the evening came to an end he thought it would be a good idea to canvass the views of the current councillors as regards his intention to put himself forward as a candidate.

Eight asked, 'who are you'?

Three asked, 'which Lyme family were you born into'?

Two enthused about new blood.

And the other one said, 'can't stop, last orders at the Nag's Head , but no comment anyway.'

Michael didn't really know what he felt after his first experience of town council life. Was he excited? Exasperated? Enraged? Or another word beginning with E he could not bring to mind. Time would tell.

Chapter Eight-Connor Gets The News

It was a bombshell there could be no denying. No more Bradley Steel, no more Judy Hamilton for that matter. He knew of course, it would happen one day. It had to, it stood to reason. He knew that, but all the same...it was a blow. The biggest blow he had received in fact since his cat Teazel and his cousin Nigel in Wath upon Dearne, in a rare display of synchronicity and downright bad timing, had died on the same day.

But why oh why did she have to kill Bradley off? He personally thought and had thought for a very long time that Judy had a mean streak, this confirmed it. True, he had done very well out of Judy Hamilton. True, he had other authors; unfortunately they were not as successful as Judy. He winced when he thought of James Galvin whose novel about a serial killer who skins his victims was flayed by the critics. Or Belinda Williams, whose charming fable about a Dorset fossiler was absolutely hammered. Not to mention Hugo Parkins, whose case history of a poltergeist haunting, that he hoped would tap into the public's fascination with the paranormal, was knocked by all. There were successes too but none to rival Judy.

He would long remember that day. The day Judy broke the news that is. Not the day that Teazel and Nigel died. Although no doubt Connor will remember that day too. It's not every day your cousin runs out in front of a car and your cat gets trapped in a reclining armchair.

"Hello Connor."

"Who is this please?"

"Oh Connor, it's Judy!"

"Oh yes, sorry Judy, the old ear wax problem again. How's the book going, almost done?"

"Yes, well actually it's finished, but you're not going to like it."

"You never know, I have liked one or two of them, well the parts I read anyway."

"Thank for the overwhelming vote of confidence, Connor."

"Hey, I publish them; I don't have to read them."

"True, I guess. Here goes, I have killed him…"

"Michael?"

"Hah! Bradley Steel is no more."

"What? Are you mad? He is my…er…I mean our bread and butter. You can't just kill him off"

"I can and I have. Connor, this is my last book, there will be no more."

"I have heard that lots of times, Judy and guess what? they all come back for a swan song."

"This swan has sung her last song. Look, Connor, I have to go now, Michael has a bottle of wine here with my name on."

"Chateau Judy, how sweet. Next time we speak, you will have seen sense I hope."

"No chance. Well, I would have seen sense obviously, as I am already seeing sense. Does that make sense?"

"Sadly, yes. Bye for now, Judy. Email me the gubbins."

"Will do. Bye."

And that was it. All over. He was perplexed, puzzled and another word beginning with P he could not quite bring to mind. Of course he would try to persuade Judy to reconsider her decision, but he was sure it would be to no avail. He would try and interest her in a new series of books featuring maybe a darts player who when not throwing arrows and working out at the gym, leads a charmed life as a private detective specialising in smashing rings of criminals who themselves specialised in the distribution of counterfeit golfing trousers, but he was sure it would be to no avail. He would prove to be right in that respect.

"I've told him," said Judy, "did you hear?"

"I was sitting right here, of course I heard."

"He took it quite well I thought."

"He might have done, but you can bet he will get busy trying to get you to change your mind."

"He can try but he won't succeed. You know me, Mike…once I have made my mind up about something that's it."

Michael did know that. More than once, he had fallen foul of Judy's determination. She had always been more driven and motivated. He had never found motivating himself easy.

"Pity the ending didn't involve closets and coming out of them"

"You can't have everything you want, Mike."

"I have you, Jude. You will do for me every time."

"Aww, Mike…my romantic hero."

"I try."

"You mostly succeed!"

"Mostly?"

"Well, you're not perfect."

Michael agreed with that. He was not perfect. Everyone said so.

"But you'll do for me," continued Judy.

He kissed her. It was the appropriate response.

Chapter Nine-Fay Takes A Trip

"That was Fay on the phone," said Judy, having just got off the phone. Obviously.

"Fay Weldon?"

"Hah!"

"How is she? We don't hear from her too much these days."

"Once every three months or so is fairly regular for Fay."

"True. What is she up to?"

"She is going to do a couple of days walking around Vågsfjorden."

"Sounds a tad chilly to me," said Michael, who had never cared for Scandinavian countries although none of them had done him any harm.

"She has been planning it for a while," said Judy.

****

'Well. I've been planning it for a while,' thought Fay as she packed her bags in her house in Harstad.

The house had been a parting gift from Stammersson Inc in gratitude for all she had done for the company while at the helm.

It suited Fay admirably. It was secluded to the point of invisibility, a state that Fay wished she could accomplish for herself. She had never been one for crowds, for cities. She had friends (very few), lovers (occasionally), but she loved her solitude. And she should find plenty of solitude on the island of Andørja which is where she was intending to do her exploring. A short boat ride on a sjark with one of the local fishermen and the wilderness would be there before her. Waiting for her.

She had always been a moderately sensible woman and had packed her rucksacks in what can only be described as a sensible manner. Andreas Esepeth was even now waiting for her, no doubt with a Norwegian gleam in his eye, for he had an often declared a soft spot for Fay as evinced by the crates of fish he often delivered to the house. Fay did rather like him, but as for a relationship; oh no. Not her type at all. Well, apart from his ruggedness and manliness, but Fay had long ago decided that didn't always count for much in her men or in the case of Steve Newsome, not at all.

Fay had not decided on her return route so did not enlist the services of Andreas which was probably just as well for the broken leg and broken arm that he suffered after becoming entangled in one of his nets after being attacked by an amorous cod, would have prevented such a pick-up.

Fay only spoke to her father every two months or so, no alarm bells would be ringing there.

Fay only spoke to Judy every six weeks or so, no alarm bells would be ringing there.

Once Andreas was able to get around a little, he cajoled his brother into taking him to Fay's Harstad house. Repeated visits bore no response.

After three months Tom was thinking it odd that Fay had not called. Judy was puzzled that Fay had left it so long to call, but this kind of lull in communication was by no means unknown.

Eventually there was a consultation with those members of the board of Stammersson Inc who had kept in contact with Fay. Action was taken. The police were empowered to effect an entry to Fay's house. It was just as she had left it that day.

Searches of the island were in vain. Fay had vanished. No trace of her was ever discovered.

Chapter Ten-Books For All

Not one of Judy's television appearances could be termed a complete success; even calling any one of them a partial success would be pushing the boundaries of the definition of success. Her one appearance (one evening-two shows) on Chapter and Verse or Worse hardly covered her in literary glory, not that the show had ever covered anyone in literary glory. Perversely, she had enjoyed the experience and was more than willing to put herself forward for guesting on future shows. No further invitation was extended to her. Life was unfair as Katy had often remarked upon in her teenage years. Staggeringly often in fact.

Still, the invitation to appear on Books For All was quite welcome. It was more of a review show than a game show and rarely for this day and age showed no signs of dumbing down its content and format. There seemed to be an unwritten law that all TV shows had to have a quiz element to them, some form of competition, and failure in such shows usually involved some form of ritual humiliation for the losers. The spirit of the age was and is winning, according to the crowded schedules.

Recording for the show was taking place in Bristol which suited Judy down to the ground; no overnight stay involved, just a quick (although not that quick) blast up and down the M5. Sorted. Michael had offered to accompany her, he was good like that. Occasions such as these made her unusually nervous and having Michael looking on would do absolutely nothing to alleviate that, if anything it would increase it.

Not an auspicious start, being stranded in reception for an hour. Unlike Michael, she was never tardy and now she paid the price, being on her third coffee (shades of Clapham Junction station that morning) and consequently even more jittery than normal. She was a great believer in punctuality in spite of the loneliness that often went hand in hand with it. One or two people strode purposefully towards her. 'This is it,' she thought, 'here we go.' But they just as purposefully strode away from her. She wisely turned down the fourth coffee that had just been offered to her by a kindly member of the reception staff. Judy was unaware of the daily sweepstake amongst the self-same reception staff as to who could serve the most coffees to unsuspecting visitors. She didn't notice the look of disappointment on the face of Hazel Wiltshire (badge-HAZEL-HERE TO HELP) who was now destined to suffer another crushing defeat.

Then, after another twenty minutes had elapsed during which Judy had perused and ultimately ignored the content of the new re-vamped Peoples Friend now being marketed and re-branded for a younger readership i.e. 60-70s, someone ambled over to her purposefully. This new arrival on the scene announced herself to Judy as Faith Addison, programme assistant.

"You're wearing that are you, love?"

"Yes," replied Judy, who had selected her dress with great care that morning; not too flashy, not too sombre. "Why, what's wrong with it?"

"I didn't say there was anything wrong with it."

"The implication was there loud and clear."

"I wasn't implying anything and I resent the implication that I was."

Faith was now thinking that this was going to be one of those days. Judy was now thinking this was going to be one of those days unless she did something about it.

"I apologise. Blame the coffee and my nerves. Can we start again?" asked Judy.

"You're wearing that are you, love?"

"Yes I am, do you like it?"

"I adore it, Mrs Hamilton."

"Please, call me Judy."

They both laughed. Equilibrium restored. Onwards and upwards.

"What do you know about the show, Judy?"

"Next to nothing, sadly."

"You've seen it of course, I assume."

"You assume wrongly, Faith. I am not a great television watcher. But I have watched a clip or two in the last week or two so I am not as green as my dress."

"Ah yes, that dress. Sorry…look I'll run through how it works and what's required of you. You know what books are being discussed today?"

"Yes and I managed to blitz through them in time."

"That's something at least."

"At least? I resent the implication there that I have somehow not done enough for this precious show."

"I wasn't implying anything and I resent the implication I was."

Damn. 'Here we go again,' they both thought.

"Can we start that bit again?" asked Judy.

"You know what books are being discussed today?"

"Yes."

"Good."

Easy as that.

The next stage in the proceedings was the meet the fellow guests stage. Michael had asked Judy earlier if she knew who her fellow guests would be. Her answer was the expected one; "No idea, your guest is as good as mine."

She was introduced to Rebecca Kuehler who was riding high in the literary world, having been nominated for various prizes and was deemed to be one of the front runners for the Booker prize. None of that particularly struck a chord with Judy, what did concern her that Rebecca (or Miss Kuehler as she preferred to be addressed) also favoured the wearing of a green dress. Somehow, Judy couldn't imagine Faith saying "You're wearing that are you, love?" to Miss Rebecca Kuehler.

"Hello Judy," said the aforementioned Miss Kuehler in a facsimile of friendliness. Then the axe fell. "I see you indulge in green too. What a sweet dress and so...*affordable*."

Judy found herself struggling to come up with a suitable response although she was thinking very much along the lines of snooty, supercilious and another word beginning with S she could not quite bring to mind. Her response when it came was not the most cutting she would ever come up with, but perfect for the arrogant Miss Rebecca Kuehler.

"Hello Becky," she said. She could have asked is it Becky with a Y or Becki with an I. She could have, but she didn't.

With a haughty look (practised daily in front of a mirror) Miss Rebecca Kuehler melted towards the complementary drinks table. To clarify, the drinks were complementary not the table.

Standing in the corner, or even slouching in the corner while this encounter was going on was the other guest, Jonathan Harle who had recently completed his epic tome, *The History of Weather Reporting in the British Isles with particular reference to precipitation.* A worthy follow up to his *Snowfall in Yorkshire from 1432 to 2000 with particular reference to Ilkley Moor.*

"Hello, I'm Jonathan," he said, quite accurately, "How are you?"

Judy replied that she was very well indeed, also quite accurately. This answer seemed to satisfy Jonathan who retreated to the corner for another bout of standing, slouching and another word beginning with S I can't quite bring to mind. A glass of wine was offered to Judy who deliberated long and hard about accepting. By the time she had deliberated and arrived at the decision to accept, the wine had already left the room. Anyway, perhaps it wouldn't have sat well with the three coffees. Ah yes, the three coffees; she was sure she had seen a toilet somewhere on her travels through the corridors. She gesticulated at Faith who was the other side of the room sharing Jonathan's corner. Faith gesticulated back. Neither one had any idea what the other one meant. You may wonder why Judy didn't just ask someone where the toilet was. That was precisely what Judy was thinking when Faith announced the show was about to start.

The format had remained the same since the show's inception several years previously. The hosts were rotated on a regular basis, sure it made them dizzy, but it kept the show fresh! The set was simple; four armchairs, upholstered in leather, a small table and behind the armchairs, a bookcase filled with what appeared to be hundreds of books, but it was all an illusion; they were all facsimiles of book spines. Even so, many viewers it is believed spend all the show trying to identify the books. Difficult of course because as we all know, you can't judge a book by its cover or even it's spine.

The host for this particular show was Rufus George who had been reviewing books for The Guardian since he was old enough to know better. His style was incisive yet avuncular, argumentative yet considerate. Jonathan Harle and the haughty Miss Rebecca Kuehler had appeared on the show before and settled down into their armchairs along the lines of greeting old friends. Not that they would necessarily greet their old friends by sitting on them, although in certain circumstances it could be distinctly possible. Judy settled back in her armchair with a degree of discomfiture that could not be wholly attributable to the armchair in question. She breathed deeply and tried the best she could to appear relaxed in spite of her nervousness and full bladder.

Rufus made the introductions to a polite ripple of applause from the invited audience, mostly made up from the ranks of writers and reviewers plus a smattering of librarians who always enjoyed a day out. Rufus then announced the first book for discussion, *Summer Repealed, Summer Repelled* by Kaitlyn Wymer, a novel of love in the Welsh Valleys set against the backdrop of coal mine closures. It had already won the Merthyr Tydfil Golden Daffodil award, the Pontypool Prize and was rumoured to be selling like hot Welsh cakes in Haverfordwest.

Judy had read it although it was fairer to say she struggled through it, finding it a tad turgid, but was she here to be honest? Or could she get by saying the nicest thing she could about it? (She liked the font). She still had a little time to decide as Jonathan was the first to be invited to air his views.

"I'm glad you asked me first, Rufus. I can hardly contain my excitement when it comes to this novel. Life-affirming is an overused phrase when it comes to reading certain books…"

Judy nodded.

"…but this work is life-affirming, even life-changing. It works on so many levels from the simple pastoral delights of the

Welsh hills to the daily grind of life. It has soul, it has power and captures the very essence of a life in which sorrow and joy walk hand in hand. The author is searingly honest in her portrayal of this fractured family. It is a remarkable piece of work."

"Thank you, Jonathan," said Rufus, who was always glad that someone actually had something to say. "Rebecca, what are your thoughts?"

"It's not often I would agree with Jonathan…"

Cue titters from the invited audience.

"…but his appreciation of this monumental work mirrors my own. What a stupendous read, full of pathos, humour and tragedy. I can't even begin to place it in any one genre; is it comedy, is it tragedy, is it kitchen-sink drama on a scale I personally have never encountered before? Of course it's all of those things. The characterisations are as sharp and multi-faceted as anything Charles Dickens ever came up with it. It is family life under the microscope revealed to us bit by bit by an author who is in total control. A true cross-genre novel of rare power."

"Well put, Rebecca. Judy, what about you?"

"What about me?"

"Er…your thoughts and insights about the novel. Did you find it hard to label, to categorise in any one genre?"

"I know of only two categories that books come into."

"Two? *Two*?" exclaimed a perplexed if not actually shocked Jeremy. "How can you say that? You'll have to tell us what these two categories of yours are."

"Those I like and those I dislike," replied Judy. "Simple."

Cue more titters from the invited audience.

"So perhaps," asked Miss Rebecca Kuehler, "you could enlighten as to whether you liked *Summer Repealed, Summer Repelled?*"

"Yes."

"Yes you liked it?" asked Rebecca

"No, I mean yes I can enlighten you, Becky."

"It's Rebecca, please do so."

"I quite liked some aspects of it."

"Care to put that into words for us?" asked Rufus.

Judy, sensing a sense of hostility from her fellow guests suddenly felt she would rather be anywhere than here. Or more precisely, she would rather be in Lyme Regis with Michael as she quite often felt when she wasn't there.

"I was under the impression I just had."

"Can we just move on please?" asked, indeed almost begged the imperious Miss Rebecca Kuehler.

"I second that," seconded Jonathan Harle.

Rufus George breathed deeply and feeling sufficiently calm, attempted to wrest back control of the show. "Perhaps we can move on to the second novel under discussion," he said, hoping there would be a discussion of sorts otherwise there was a distinct possibility they would be ending twenty-three minutes early. Unthinkable.

"Yes, let's do that," replied Jonathan.

"I hope you all enjoyed reading this extraordinary novel as much as I did."

Jonathan nodded. Miss Rebecca Kuehler nodded. Judy shook her head.

The novel in question was, *The Daemon Child*, a haunting tale of possession in Victorian London. This was the debut novel of Stephen Bello, who had turned away from teaching to become a writer and was now reaping the rewards. There were hints of a film version, even a television series.

"I have never been so, if I may be permitted to use the word, possessed by a novel as I was by *The Daemon Child*. Every time I picked the book up it was as though icy fingers were encircling my neck and puncturing my heart…"

"Big hand was it, Becky?" observed Judy. "Sorry."

"…to read it was to know exactly how it must feel to have your very soul in danger of eternal suffering. Stephen Bello seems to be a natural master of creating atmosphere which is both claustrophobic and inviting. By that I mean he invites the reader in, in order to turn the screws in a veritable crescendo of fear."

Jonathan waded in. "Interesting you should refer, even obliquely, to *The Turn of the Screw*, for that is the very novel I was forcibly reminded of. Stephen gets under your skin in much the same way as Henry James did with his account of Miles and Flora. I was unsettled by it and I can tell you here and now that sleep did not come easily for a few nights and when it did, I made sure the light stayed on. I don't normally read anything which even resembles a horror novel and for anyone watching who may feel the same, I say embrace this book, love this book, but be prepared to go on a journey into the darkest recesses of the human psyche."

"Thank you, Jonathan, great insights. Judy?"

"I liked it."

"Er...great," responded a clearly exasperated Rufus. He was almost, but not quite, lost for words. "Could you perhaps tell us how much you liked it?"

"Oh, very much!"

Rufus George knew at that moment that all was lost. He stumbled on. They all stumbled on save for Judy who was revelling in her performance. She was good at pricking pomposity in others. Everyone said so. Unfortunately, no one would know on this particular occasion for when the director yelled cut, it was permanent. The show was abandoned. Judy was both cold-shouldered and abandoned. Did she care? No.

It is a well-known fact in the Hamilton family home that Michael always had too much time on his hands. It must be true because Judy said so. This time, Michael had latterly been using to explore music that he may have and indeed had missed the first time around. Particularly the music of the seventies as recommended by their new neighbour, Andy Burton, a guitarist of note who made his name, but not his fame in various progressive rock bands of a slightly later era. That era was the echo of the original era of progressive rock when music was ponderous, portentous and another word beginning with P I cannot quite bring to mind.

Michael's exploration of seventies music was not just confined to progressive rock; it took in the music which adorned the charts too. Progressive rock bands whilst crowding the album charts, were unable to crack the singles market…even after severe editing the shortest playing time for any one song was on average nine minutes and thirty-seven seconds. He had an infuriating habit for days on end (along with his other habits) of singing John Miles's biggest hit, *Music*. 'Music was my first love…' could be heard all over the house. This of course was palpable nonsense for his first love was undeniably Sarah Higginson with whom he had frolicked all over the Cotswolds or at least the parts of the Cotswolds that were accessible on foot. They were particularly familiar with several hayricks of that area. Sorry, John Miles and music.

Judy never actually did anything quite as precise as timing the various solos that progressive rock was seemingly built on, but she quite often found that she could run a bath, luxuriate in it with a good book, clean the bath out, dress and still be back with Michael before the guitar solo came to an end.

On one memorable (although not that memorable) occasion, she left Michael listening to *Storms Over Mars At Dawn* by The Ebbing Tide. The drummer, Kurt Coughlan was just beginning the drum solo which formed the climax of the song. Judy drove to Axminster, did the weekly shop, had a coffee in one of the numerous coffee shops, drove back to Lyme after filling up the tank at Uplyme Filling Station and arrived as Kurt completed the final triple diddle, finishing with a telling cymbal crash.

"Is that the same, the very same drum solo?"

"Yes, Jude, magnificent isn't it?"

"I don't think I would describe it in quite those terms, no. Didn't the musicians and I use the word advisedly, ever get bored? Did anyone ever fall asleep? And if they did, did anyone notice?"

"Are you being *crotchet*y?"

"Only because it doesn't strike a *chord* with me."

"Keep calm, Jude, don't lose your *tempo*!"

"Ouch. I don't suppose you would *fret* about it if I did."

"I wouldn't exactly, but you might be in the right *aria*."

"I am going to *beat* you again, you will just fade out."

"I think word plays are becoming my *forte*."

"You be careful you don't fall *flat*, Mike."

"Don't *harp* on about it."

"No need to, Mike, I am going to *waltz* away with this one."

"I am so confident that if you do win I'll give you a tenor."

"I'll make a *note* of that."

"Very *sharp* of you."

"Anything to help restore *harmony*."

"Er…..um…….damn!"

Musical interlude over.

Chapter Twelve-Politics For All, Well Not Quite All

Surprisingly enough, Michael's experiences at local council meetings had not in any way dampened his enthusiasm for partaking in local government. His enthusiasm had yet to be matched by any kind of policy, but he was confident that would come. More rights for ghosts? Sponsored word plays? Tax relief for dodgy knees? The reality was that all he wanted was to do his best for the town, to ensure it was a town with something for everyone where no one was excluded on any grounds, where the youth of the town were involved in all aspects of the town's economic and social life. He wanted to give something back to this wonderful place which had become home.

It was almost a policy; at least it came from the heart. Wheels were put in motion. People who should be notified were notified. People who needed to know were told. People were canvassed again, with the same mixed results as before. He sent his 'blurb' to the printers along with a suitable photograph that had been selected with care by Judy. One thousand, five hundred leaflets were duly printed and delivered. There was a fly in the electioneering ointment.

"Mike, are you aware that those leaflets should have your name and address printed on them?"

"Really?"

"No, I just said that to waste your time for the hell of it. Did you not check the small print on the nomination papers?"

"Apparently not," he replied and instantly wished he hadn't, but not instantly enough. "Sorry, Jude. No, I must have missed that."

"You will also have missed the fact that to omit it, will render the whole election null and void, should someone complain."

"I reckon we will get away with it. By the way does the term null ever get used on its own? I've always wondered that."

"You are forgetting that this is Lyme Regis, you can't get away with anything let alone using null without void. Someone will always complain and it will be your undoing."

"I have always preferred you to be my undoing, Jude."

"That's as maybe, but it won't get you elected. Our options are, have the leaflets reprinted, pull out of the election or..."

"Write it on ourselves!" concluded Michael.

"*Our*selves?"

"You are my campaign manager after all."

"Since when?"

Michael smiled his 'you can't resist me' smile and performed his very best Gallic shrug.

"Campaign manager eh? I like the sound of that. Clearly, I am in charge, but it's good to hear you acknowledge it even if you came up with that on the spur of the moment to enlist my help in writing your name and address on *fifteen hundred* leaflets."

Another Gallic shrug seemed the appropriate response.

"Come on then, I'll help."

"Thanks, Jude. Shall I put some music on?"

"That will be your music I assume. It might be a good idea."

Michael kept quiet as he knew there would be a further comment. He was right.

"Hmm, let me think…fifteen hundred leaflets? That would equate to three guitar solos and two and a half drum solos unless either of us needs to go to the toilet in which case we will need the full three drum solos plus a saxophonist and a tinkling triangle."

"All I can say to that is, if you hadn't been so thorough and actually read the small print we would have been blissfully ignorant and could have spent the evening engaged in other activities," said Michael in a rare display of bravery.

Judy surprisingly took it in good humour despite the onerous task ahead.

"That's what a campaign manager is for. Anyway as for other activities, I can multi-task and drink wine at the same time. A large glass of Pinot Grigio if you please."

"I love it when you pretend to misunderstand me."

"You will love me all the more in fifteen hundred leaflets' time."

Michael handed over a pile of leaflets to Judy along with a pen and they set to it. The hours ticked by and then ticked by some more. The hours turned to more hours. One o' clock in the morning arrived as Judy departed for bed. Michael girded his loins (not literally, that would be hideous) and persevered. At two-fifteen, he could no longer remember his name let alone write it. Thirty minutes later he had no idea where he lived. Fifteen minutes after that he too was in bed. At six in the morning, refreshed by hardly any sleep he set to work again. At eight o' clock he scrawled his address on the final leaflet.

Judy appeared soon afterwards and gazed at the piles of leaflets adorning the dining table, the sofa and hearth. Looking at the paperwork that came from the district council, she pulled a face which momentarily puzzled Michael, but only for as long as it took Judy to tell him the reason for the look on her face.

"Mike, you are supposed to have the printer's name and address on them too."

"What, you are kidding?"

She wasn't.

"And are they not there?"

They weren't.

Michael let out a scream which would have travelled as far as Monkton Wyld had there been a stiff sea-breeze and they hadn't been inside. Five hours and five large coffees later the leaflets were deemed ready for delivery.

"Do you think I should kiss any babies if we encounter any?"

"No, I don't think you should kiss anyone at all let alone babies."

"How about you?"

"I won't be kissing anyone either."

"I didn't mean that, Jude."

"I know that, my teasable hero."

He kissed her; it was as ever the appropriate response.

They had allowed themselves three days to cover the whole of Lyme Regis, wisely taking dodgy knees and the occasional cider into consideration. The weather had been behaving itself perfectly for days, but the moment Michael and Judy set off, the heavens opened. The rain could best be described as pitiless; it was almost malignant in its intensity. Colway Lane gave in all too easily and became a raging torrent of a river. They were convinced and probably quite rightly, that they had never been so drenched in their lives although they remembered a particular Monday in Venice. That was a memorable afternoon of rain…and other delights. Well, it was their honeymoon.

A change of clothes and back they came for round two. Michael only complained seven times about his dodgy knees. If it had not been in a good cause it would have been double that easily. There seemed to be an abundance of dogs that had been clearly positioned behind the letter-boxes of various homes in order to pounce on unsuspecting fingers that strayed into their domain. It was marginal whether the spring-loaded letter-boxes or spring-loaded jaws inflicted the most damage. Michael, far from being given a chance to expound on his aims for his tenure as a councillor was mistaken for a Jehovah's Witness three times, once for a Mormon, three times for a meter reader, once for an encyclopaedia salesman (yes they still exist) and thirteen times for another candidate. Judy fared somewhat better, she was only mistaken for an Avon lady (yes they still exist) five times.

He was asked some pointed yet not always relevant questions:

"Are you really standing for council?"

"Where in Lyme were you born?"

"You're married to that writer aren't you?"

"Didn't I see you in a fish costume in the carnival?"

"But you read my meter last week didn't you?"

"Could you screw this light bulb in for me?"

His answers were as succinct as they could possibly be; Yes, I wasn't, Yes, No, No and Yes. It wasn't local politics as he had envisaged, but these were early days. He was on his way.

After two further days of intermittent rain, painful knees and bitten fingers all the leaflets were delivered. Now he could sit back and await the feedback. He had a piece printed in two local newspapers outlining his aims and expectations. He sat back and awaited the feedback. The feedback was muted to the point of non-existence. He was not worried, that sort of setback didn't bother him. Everyone said so.

When polling day came around, Michael was up early for a day of canvassing in the town, on the seafront and in one or two pubs. He felt better able to discuss his aims and expectations with a cider or three inside him. The vote was counted at Woodmead Hall and Michael by this time was confident that he had put up a good show. The net result of this confidence, intense canvassing and exhausting leaflet delivery was a paltry twenty-three votes. Twenty-three.

"How did you do, Michael?" asked Andy Burton the following day.

"Last. Twenty-three votes."

Andy considered this for a moment or two. "How many people do you know in Lyme?"

"Apparently, twenty-three!"

Michael, although dejected was not put off by this poor showing and stood for council a few more times, polling 112, 48, 101, 129, 56 and 68 votes.

Then he gave up. Judy was somewhat disappointed as she thought Michael would have made an excellent councillor. She knew he had numerous talents hidden up his sleeve…well hidden, but there all the same. She thought sitting on the council would help him realise what she already knew about him. She also enjoyed the leaflet deliveries as it took her back to her teenage years as a newspaper girl in the lanes of Surrey; the rain, the mud, the dogs and the challenge of getting the Saturday papers through a letterbox the size of…well, a letterbox. It was as character building as one could get in East Molesey.

Chapter Thirteen-Feet, Knees And Other Joints (No Not That Sort)

"Is it your knees again?" asked a freshly materialised Captain Edward De Vere Fox.

"No, why do you ask?"

"It's quite usual to find you relaxing on the…the…what is it again?"

"It's a patio, Captain."

"Yes, yes so it is…where was I?"

"Relaxing."

"Was I?"

"No, I was."

"Ah yes. My point was that it is usually your knees or back that drive you to rest on this…er…thing."

"Not this time."

"Can you see my feet, dear boy?"

"Your feet?"

"Yes, can you see them?"

"Yes, of course."

"They don't happen to appear hazy to you?"

"Now you come to mention it…"

"They do?"

"They don't!"

"I am most relieved to hear it. I was beginning to have nightmares about slowly disappearing until I am left with only my head on show. Life…well…you know what I mean, would become intolerable if that were to be the case. Of course it would be ideal for purposes of haunting and scaring folk to Kingdom come, but that is not what it's all about is it?"

Michael wasn't too sure how to answer, never having been dead and therefore never having felt the need to haunt anyone even if he had wanted to. Which he didn't.

"I suppose not, Captain. Perhaps this haziness where your feet are concerned is just an illusion."

"I'd like to believe that, I really would dear boy, but young Thomas is similarly affected; his hands are fading away and young Thomas is very fond of his hands. You no doubt recall the incident involving Judy's sister, Michael."

"I do indeed."

Fay had been touched by young Thomas. By the stream if you please. And this on her first visit to the Old House. Young Thomas had been quick to absolve himself by telling the captain that Fay Kennedy was the most beautiful woman he had seen since encountering Eleanor Framble, a farmer's daughter of Kineton who had educated him in…country ways.

"Well, sorry to burden you with my problems, dear boy."

"No problem at all, Captain."

"Farewell for now then," said the captain as he faded away.

74

Michael, on the whole was generally truthful, but he thought it better not to tell the captain that he couldn't see his feet. It seemed unkind somehow.

Chapter Fourteen-A Birthday Party, Tom At Eighty

It was agreed by all that it should be low key. It was agreed by all that it could not possibly be a celebration under the circumstances. It was agreed by all, however, that this particular birthday had to be noted somehow. Tom was never one to be made a fuss of and turning eighty was never going to change that. Reluctant as he was to be the centre of attention and being the centre of attention is obligatory as far as birthdays are concerned, he agreed to a small get-together which was to be held at his Coburg Terrace home.

The woman who 'did' for him, Pamela Bowers was on hand before during and after the event to aid in its smooth running. Michael and Judy both liked her and fortunately so did Tom. Pamela had overseen many a birthday party and her catering skills were second to none. Everyone said so. Tom had even agreed to Pamela baking a lemon drizzle cake to Elspeth's carefully protected recipe. Pamela wanted to do justice to Elspeth's lemon drizzle cakes and she knew she could. She loved baking, indeed, she had reached the final of The Great Devon Baking Stars held in a converted school building in Exeter. She should have won, she knew that, but her nerves let her down and her showstopper 'octopus cake' was missing three tentacles and several grammes of sugar. Not her finest moment and she wisely never attempted another octopus cake, something she has in common with almost everyone in Devon. Her dilemma was whether to pull out all the stops and come up with something that may be better than Elspeth's creations or rein herself in and play it safe. For Tom's sake she decided to rein herself in.

Katy was away touring. Annabelle was just away. Michael and Judy after a gentle awakening drove over to Sidmouth for ten o' clock. Judy had made a birthday cake two days before. Michael watched. He was good like that. He was also good at licking out bowls when they were offered to him, something he had become accustomed to as a boy and he saw no need whatsoever to alter this characteristic in spite of advancing years. What's the point of being older if you can't be younger occasionally? Or often.

That's not to say he hadn't made himself useful for he had. He had personally selected and bought the crisps and the pork scratchings that he was both confident and hopeful no one else would be wanting, but him. He had personally selected and bought the wines and the cider that he was both confident and hopeful no one else would be wanting, but him. He didn't always find shopping easy unless it was for himself.

Pamela had attended to the rest of the food and had spent an extra hour cleaning the house and re-arranging the furniture to accommodate the guests. She didn't go as far as lifting the carpets. It wasn't that type of party. A few of Tom's friends from the bowling club had been invited, some of them had even accepted.

Fay had been expected to fly into the country two days earlier and then come to Axminster by train from Waterloo. Repeated phone calls to Fay's home in Harstad went unanswered; it had been several weeks since Michael and Judy had heard from her, that in itself was not unusual, but this was different, it was her father's 80th and it was hard to imagine what had kept her from attending. She was her own woman though; she had demonstrated that often over the years.

Understandably, it was Tom's first thought when he greeted them at the door.

"No Fay?"

"No, Dad. We don't know what's happened; perhaps there has been a problem with the flight or something."

"Then she would have called wouldn't she? You mark my words, Judy, there will be a man somewhere behind this. You know what she's like. She always craved excitement while you settled for Michael."

"Thanks, Tom!"

"No offence, Michael."

"None taken. Much."

"Whatever it is, Dad, I'm sure it's nothing to worry about."

"Depends on how you define worry. She's not here and we can't do anything about it so come in, eat drink and be merry for tomorrow…"

It was a sentence that perhaps Tom should not have started and definitely one he could not finish; the pain of losing Elspeth was still too raw.

Pamela greeted them at the bottom of the stairs with a cheery hello and an even cheerier drink, in this case lime and soda which diluted the cheeriness somewhat. Pamela had very firm and deeply entrenched ideas about the times that alcohol could and should be drunk and this time of day was most definitely a soft drinks time of day. Not that it mattered to Judy; she was driving as was usually the case when the family event was one that involved her family. Michael could bide his time even though he didn't always find biding his time easy. But he felt that Johnny Norfolk could easily wait a while before propping up the bar at the Barton United club house and surely Johnny Stevens would be in no rush to get the drinks in S*P*Y*S the fashionable club for 'government operatives' in Curzon Street.

A knock at the door heralded the arrival of several senior members (they were about as senior as you could get) of the Sidmouth Bowling Club. They handled Pamela's alcohol rule with a great deal of stiff upper lip fortitude and the odd sip from various hip flasks none of which contained lime and soda.

Introductions were made. Names duly forgotten. A close eye was kept on the clock. Or several eyes actually. Pamela kept a close eye on the eyes and the clock. Tom's bowling friends were a mixed bunch, as much as you can be a mixed bunch with a minimum age of seventy-two and a maximum age of eighty-eight. They seemed inordinately proud of the creases in their trousers; to a man, razor sharp. They seemed inordinately proud of the length of their trousers; to a man, two inches above their highly polished shoes. It had been years since Michael had seen so many neckties assembled in one place. You could say many things about the Sidmouth Bowling Club members (although not that many), but you could not deny that they were always nicely turned out. Sidmouth in fact was a hotbed of blazer sales in Britain, not forgetting slacks.

Jack Rodwell was busy trying to convert Michael to the delights of crown green bowling, something even Tom had never mastered. The delights in question seemed to be questionable and Michael's head was spinning with talk of forfeited bowls, dead bowls, strikes, standard jacks and running jacks. Presumably not Jack Rodwell whose running days were surely long past.

"And Michael, you can bring along the little woman."

Michael looked around in feigned surprise and puzzlement.

"Which one, Jack?"

"Your wifey."

"She does have a name you know."

"Of course, of course, but I don't know it."

"I introduced you to her only a few moments ago."

"Sorry I am not very good with women's names. Men's names tickety boo, but women's names, tricky coves."

There seemed no suitable response to this and as it was now three minutes past twelve, Michael went in search of a cider. He found one. He was good like that.

Tom was amiable, amenable and another word beginning with A I can't quite bring to mind. While he was not quite the life and soul of the party, not that anyone expected him to be, at least he was functioning to the best of his ability. The grief which still consumed him was held at bay for a day. And day to day living was how Tom held his life together. He had suffered from severe depression during his 'time of trouble' as the Molesey WI termed it when having stern words with Elspeth concerning Tom's alleged 'dodgy dealing' when he was something big in the city. Functioning normally became totally foreign to Tom, but gradually with the help of Elspeth, Fay and Judy he came back to 'life' and in a total change of direction became something big in floristry. This extreme grief was something unknown to Tom although he had of course lost parents, close family members and friends over the years, but this all-consuming grief was foreign to him, he could not and perhaps did not want to deal with it. He still expected Elspeth to walk through the door or for him to come downstairs and find her in the kitchen baking one of her renowned creations. Most days, he could smell her perfume, hear her voice and catch the bustle of her movement throughout the house. That of course was not enough; he could conjure her up, but could not bring her back.

Tom smiled. "Thank you to everyone for making me feel special."

Cue murmurs of 'you are special' from assorted guests.

Tom continued. "You all put up with me so well and I want to let you all know how much I appreciate it. I owe Pamela a big, big thank you for working above and beyond the call of duty and for making this day go so smoothly, especially after twelve!"

Cue muted laughter and an embarrassed look on Pamela's face.

"I know I have not been much fun to be around recently, perhaps I never was."

Cue exaggerated nodding from Judy coupled with a look of concern.

"If you all have a drink in your hands, ah, I see you do..."

Cue more exaggerated nodding from the assembly with the exception of Pamela Bowers whose only experience of alcohol had, or almost certainly contributed, to her getting into 'trouble' many, many, many years ago. Although the blame could be equally split between alcohol and Andrew Bowers, who at least did the decent thing in spite of both their reservations.

"Please join me in toasting absent friends; first of all to the love of my life, Elspeth."

Glasses were raised. Drinks quaffed.

"And to my lovely daughter, Fay. Sorry, Judy, I'm not saying you aren't lovely too because you are and I'm not saying that Fay is lovelier than you because she isn't although..."

Cue a laugh or two and a bemused look from Judy.

"I am very proud of my two daughters. Fay had a hugely successful career becoming CEO of Stammersson. Inc. and Judy of course became a hugely successful author. Judy, do you remember what I said to you when you told me you wanted to write?"

"Yes, you said, 'to whom?'.

Cue another laugh or two.

"Correct, I was quick as ever on the uptake. And to my lovely granddaughters, Katy and Annabelle. Katy is away touring, she is an actress you know. Well, of course some of you do know. And to Annabelle who is away…er…"

"Just away, Dad," said Judy, helping out. She was good like that.

"Away. Er…that's it. Can I sit down now?"

Cue murmurs of 'you are sitting down already.' Indeed he was.

"Oh yes," said Tom, his turn now to have a bemused look on his face. "I seem to be permanently confused these days, but I'll tell you what, I have a good few years left in me yet!"

He had only one. Ironically, he was mown down by a florist's van, speeding to a bouquet emergency. At least it was as sudden as it was unexpected.

Chapter Fifteen-Annabelle Comes Home

How was it?

Great thanks, Mum and I have…

Got news for us?

Yes.

You're not…?

No, Dad.

What is it then?

Let me finish then…

Please do.

I have met a man.

A real one?

Thanks for that, Dad.

Who is he?

His name his Stefan.

Where is he from?

Throdnall.

Throdnall?

Yes, Throdnall.

Does that mean?

What?

That Australia is…

Off? Yes, Mum.

Good.

Good?

Yes, good.

Didn't you want me to go?

Yes, of…

Course?

Yes, of course.

But now I am not going, it's suddenly good?

Yes, of…

Course?

Yes. How did you meet?

At Katy's show, in fact…

Yes?

She was sort of seeing him?

Sort of?

Yes, Dad, sort of.

Zak Curry all over again…

I was just a …

Child?

Yes, of…

Course?

Yes. I was sort of seeing someone too.

In Banbury?

Yes.

What happened to him?

Well…

Yes?

Katy is seeing him now.

What?

Yes. It's …

Bizarre?

Yes. But…

Good?

Too, yes.

When do we…

Meet him?

Yes.

I have invited him down in two weeks. Is that…

Okay?

Yes.

Good. You will like him.

Let's hope so.

You will. He makes me feel content, cheerful and…

Another word beginning with C you can't quite bring to mind?

Yes. How did you know?

Now then, young lady…

Speech time, Dad?

Yes, of…

Course?

Yes. What are your plans now?

Do you mean…

Work? Yes.

I'll get a job. Obviously.

So simple. Doing what?

I am going to join the police force, Mum.

And she did. Just like that.

Chapter Sixteen-A Sunny Day In Lyme Regis

"Come on, Mike, let's drag ourselves down to the sea front."

"What, with these knees?"

"Hah! Do you know what the weather will do?"

"Of course. I am the king of meteorology."

"Really and how long have you been *raining*?"

"Long enough to take the *wind* out of your sails, Jude."

"All *hail* the king is it?"

"Very much so. Tell you what; I am so confident of winning this one so on the off chance I do lose I will bake a lemon *drizzle* cake for us."

"That will just put you under *pressure!*"

"Not this time; it's you who will feel the *heat.*"

"I don't care *weather* you think that or not. It won't be long before you are down in the *doldrums* and you exit this word play under a *cloud.*"

"There is *snow* way I am going to lose; I'm going to get the win that is *dew* to me!"

"You think you are going to steal my *thunder* do you?"

"Yes and you will have to *shower* me with compliments."

"You put yourself under *pressure*, Mike and later when you realise you have mist out you will only have yourself to blame. Pride *precipitates* a fall you know."

"You used pressure twice. Disqualification. A win for me."

"By default!"

"Still a win, Jude."

Judy did not argue the point, merely agreed. She was good like that. Eventually she wheedled the forecast from Michael; sunny and warm was the view of the Met Office and more worryingly, the Daily Express. Packing for the sea front was easy; a couple of cans of cider each, a book each and a smile each. Strolling along the sea front in Lyme is one of life's great pleasures. The scenery, the sights, the sounds and another word beginning with S I can't quite bring to mind. So little goes on, but so much takes place. The forecast was accurate for this was the warmest summer's day since the last warmest summer's day. In fact, on this particular summer's day, Lyme Regis was deemed to be warmer than several other locations which all shared one fact in common; for 364 days of the year, they were warmer than Lyme. Not that any of that matters when Lyme bursts into life and welcomes visitors to sample its delights. Michael had always been one for sampling delights. Everyone said so.

And after all the years they had now spent in Lyme they still sometimes had the ability to see it afresh. Michael still let out an involuntary 'wow' when looking at the view of Lyme as he drove down Charmouth Road. Judy was often heard to exclaim 'beautiful' when driving into Lyme via the Sidmouth Road. Unless she was by herself, in which case no-one heard the exclamation, but we can all imagine it. The same applies, of course, to Michael's drives down Charmouth Road. These routes are not set in stone and sometimes it is Judy who is found motoring and exclaiming in

Charmouth Road and Michael doing something uncannily similar in Sidmouth Road.

The seafront was as busy as they had seen it in recent years; certainly since the turnstiles and ticketing system had been abandoned. Dorset and Devon had been experiencing a surge in tourist numbers ever since Cornwall proclaimed independence. The county was now suffering an economic backlash and moves were afoot to turn the clock back; a devolution revolution.

The Cart Road's new 'moving walkway' was working a like a dream, carrying whole families and brave seagulls towards the waiting pubs and fast food outlets. There was still to be heard the occasional cry of, 'look there's the Isle of Wight' in spite of the large neon signs stating clearly, 'THAT IS PORTLAND ACTUALLY'. The beaches were cleaner than at any time Michael and Judy could remember. Many years ago there had been a total ban on dogs being walked on any of the beaches. Later this was extended to become a total ban on dogs within a two mile radius of Lyme to the enormous benefit of all. Apart from dog lovers.

It was difficult deciding whether Lyme was more user-friendly now or less. It depended on the users and the degree of friendliness they perceived. As far as Michael and Judy were concerned, Lyme, whatever its faults were was still a perfect place to live and to bring up children. Everyone said so.

Michael was sipping his cider manfully out of his plastic glass. He didn't find rushing cider easy. A good thing of course. A seagull had temporarily shattered the peace on the adjoining table and was in process of making off with a leg of lamb. It was a particularly strong specimen, but even so, pursuit came easy to the other thirty-eight seagulls which flew as one after it. By the time the leg of lamb dropped into the sea ten minutes later, the thrill of the chase had worn off, being adjudged hard work when there were ample pickings on the beach.

"Do you remember our first time, Jude?"

"Your place wasn't it? Or was it mine? I take it I was there."

"Behave. Not that first time, our first time here."

"Yes, the walk from Uplyme across the fields and the wallaby!"

"Ah yes, the wallaby. I remember how excited the girls were when we reached the seafront. It felt like home already."

"What's brought on this nostalgic mood?"

"I suppose it's Katy and Annie growing up and living their own lives, it just makes me wonder about the future."

"I think our future will be much the same as our recent past unless your dodgy knees play a part."

"What about the house?"

"What about it?"

"It will be just us…"

"No, Mike. A definite no. That's our home you are talking about…"

"Almost talking about, Jude."

"I'll grant you that. Can you imagine ever leaving it? Well, can you?"

Actually, he couldn't. In fact, they wouldn't, but that's for later.

"Besides, what would the captain say?"

"You are right, Jude." Unlike many other aspects of his life he always found agreeing with Judy easy. "The captain and his men…and woman are a consideration of course. I can't imagine they would take too kindly to having another family foisted on them. Mind you, I am not too sure how long they will be around; they seem to be getting more distant with every passing day. Hazy, almost transparent."

"You've noticed that too?"

"Obviously."

Another cider for each of them. A bag of pork scratchings for Michael. Judy drew the line at such snacks although she was perfectly willing to go along with lime and rhubarb flavour crisps which really was an acquired taste, acquired by few. And still the tourists kept on coming, in search of sun, sea, sand and another delight beginning with S that I can't quite bring to mind. Their voracious appetites were sated by the culinary feasts on offer; copious amounts of fish and chips, burgers, ice-cream, pork scratchings, but very few packets of lime and rhubarb crisps. When Michael and Judy headed back along the Cart Road they found it necessary to execute the 'Lyme body-swerve' a skill which takes years to master. Needless to say, Michael had not mastered it. Judy had. It consists of scanning the approaching hordes, deciding which way they were going along with their wayward children if they had any and wayward, but artfully concealed dogs, if they had any and then at the last moment picking the gap you are going to head into, executing that perfect 'Lyme body-swerve'. Now, this requires nerves of steel and no small amount of skill. The balance and distribution of body weight has to be perfect. The steely glint in the eye has to be…well…steely, the movement swift, uncomplicated and determined. One moment you are there, the next gone with tourists trailing in your wake. Of course, Michael's knees tended to preclude such sudden movements and consequently Judy tended to leave both assorted tourists and Michael in her wake.

"I never get tired of this, Jude, being here, the view, the people."

"There is nowhere quite like it is there?"

"The best move we ever made."

"No arguments here."

"Good. Home?"

"Home."

Chapter Seventeen-Sixty!!

The fateful day had finally arrived. Michael Arkle Hamilton was sixty years old. How did he feel? Surprisingly good. For one thing, he had always been confident about reaching this age so it was a positive feeling to know his confidence had not been misplaced. He was happy with life, something he had never found easy. He was content. Incredibly so.

We can tick off his boxes of contentment one by one. Marriage to Judy. Living in Lyme Regis. Two lovely daughters, Katy and Annabelle . And now their new boyfriends, Jake and Stefan ⅓ (He wasn't too sure of them yet). There was talk of marriage however so another ⅓. A lovely house Phantoms in the garden . All in all, life was rather good.

He had not been sure about holding a party; he was always worried that no guests would turn up so he went for the option of not inviting many. He wanted a small affair; he had never found large affairs easy. He had nearly finalised his plans for this grand occasion to be held at the Woodmead Hall when Judy informed him that it was actually taking place at the Marine Theatre where a band had been laid on. A band that was guaranteed to please Michael and would be of enormous benefit to the bar takings as Judy envisaged everyone making their way there during one of the interminable guitar solos.

The first celebration of the day was certainly a small affair, consisting of two people only; Michael and Judy, who celebrated the event in the time-honoured fashion.

"Bloody hell, Mike," gasped Judy, "talk about turning the clock back."

Michael's response was a little slow coming, panting for breath as he was. But when it was came it was simple and also a throwback to earlier times, "Wow, you!"

"You're still the best, Mike."

"I was going to say that."

"That you are the best?"

"No, you are the best!"

"That's sorted then, my sixty year old hero."

"Hey, hold on....what do you mean still?"

"Figure of speech you silly man. Come on let's get downstairs before every one wonders what we have been doing."

Downstairs were Katy and Jake, accompanied by Annabelle and Stefan, who all knew exactly what Michael and Judy had been doing. Judy looked sheepish on arrival in the kitchen, Michael just a tiny bit smug.

"I thought you guys would have learned to be quieter over the years. At least it was mercifully…"

"Thank you, Katy, there's no need to embarrass poor Jake and Stefan."

"Or you, Dad!"

"Especially not me, darling."

'Happy Birthdays' rang out around the kitchen. It was decided that it was far too early for cake, but just about the perfect time for a celebratory bacon sandwich. In spite of being the birthday boy Michael was despatched to the frying pan. His bacon sandwiches were the finest for miles around, everyone said so. Well, not everyone, but certainly everyone who had partaken.

From the garden came the sound of discordant singing. It sounded like 'Happy Birthday to you' but no one was really sure. Stefan and Jake had become accustomed to the sights, sounds and hazy figures which populated the garden. Everyone looked out the window and then made for the door. In a semi-circle were a few of those self-same hazy figures including Captain Edward de Vere Fox, more prominent than the rest of the group. The never, ever seen Irish Meg contributed a lilting contralto which spoke to every one of the Emerald Isle.

"Thanks, folks," shouted Michael, "very nice."

Bacon sandwiches served. Coffee and tea poured. Stefan and Jake in addition to becoming accustomed to the various sights, sounds, shapes that popped up in the garden had also visibly relaxed in the company of Michael and Judy. And Michael and Judy for their part had become rather fond of the pair allowing for the natural reservations that parents have as part of the protection process. Still seated at the table Katy and Annabelle seemed to have reverted to their childhood, nudging each other, pulling faces and whispering. Fortunately for Annabelle's shins this throwback to earlier times did not include Katy kicking her sister.

"We have something we want to run by you," said Katy. "We are thinking about a double event."

Judy flashed Michael a look which was lost on him. Michael flashed back a look which Judy knew only too well. Judy gave the girls a knowing, expectant look. Michael didn't.

"A double event?" queried Michael, who had visions of all kinds going on his head.

"Oh come on, Dad. A double wedding."

"A double wedding? What, you and Annie?"

"No, the girls next door. Yes, us of course."

"It's not too soon maybe? It's only been a few months after all. Not that we have anything against Stefan and Jake," said Michael, managing to make it sound like they did have something against them.

"And how long was it after you met Mum that you proposed?"

"That was different, Annie."

"How?"

"Er…um…"

Judy took over as she often did. "Have you a date in mind?"

"We haven't thought that far ahead to be honest. I think Annie wants to get her latest course in full swing first."

Annabelle had sailed through the IPLDP with colours that were airborne almost from the start, the four induction levels being completed with almost obscene speed culminating in her reaching the Level 3 Diploma in Policing in record time, being fast-tracked at every turn. Her leadership qualities had been spotted and nurtured through the HPDS and inspectorship beckoned. She would eventually become the youngest superintendent since records began.

"Katy is right so maybe in a year's time would be about right and none of us has any ideas about where we want to live."

"I'll start saving straight away then!"

"Oh Dad, we won't need your money," Katy said.

"You might just get it anyway, young lady. Now, is this the point in the proceedings where I have to ask Stefan and Jake about their prospects etc?"

"No it bloody isn't, Mike. Just go and do the washing-up. We are pleased for both of you and proud of you aren't we, you there with the marigolds on?"

"Of course. Too early for champagne do you think?"

"Yes, Mike, but that has never stopped us has it?"

"True."

Champagne bottle opened. Glasses filled. Toasts made. Michael was rapidly coming to the conclusion that this was turning into a very good birthday indeed. He was quick like that. Everyone said so.

Judy and the girls had things to attend to at the theatre so Michael playing the part of prospective father-in-law decided the proper course of action was to buy Stefan and Jake a drink or two. They concurred completely and sensed that Michael didn't find buying prospective son-in-laws a drink easy. It turned into a leisurely afternoon for all concerned with the exception of Judy, Katy and Annabelle who were intent on the myriad of jobs that need to be done to ensure any party goes smoothly. Bunting doesn't hang itself you know.

The three men achieved an acceptable level of bonding during their mini drinking session. Stefan and Jake both felt they knew Michael just a little better and liked him all the more for it. Fortunately for future family relations, Michael felt the same way. And he didn't mention prospects once. Although he wanted to.

The guest list for the evening was a little on the small side, but included a few friends and especially the twenty-three people who had voted for Michael in his first attempt to win a seat on the town council, even though four of those had mistaken him for someone else. He chose not to track down and invite the one hundred and twelve people who had voted for him in his last failed attempt. Had he but known it then, he may well have thrown in the towel for there were to be five more unsuccessful bouts of electioneering. He then decided local politics was not for him.

The band, Canterbury Tales had been sound checking since four o'clock. The feedback from Robin Latimer's lead guitar had scared away every seagull for miles around and had caused a minor landslip behind the theatre. A hint of things to come. The band eschewed modern technology and relied instead on the mighty mellotron of yesteryear for their other worldly effects. They had just released their thirty-eighth album, none of which had ever graced the album charts. It had the snappy title of *The Land Where My Dreams Come From Has Now Merged With Yours* and snappy songs such as the eleven minutes and forty-eight seconds long, *Mother Earth Has Left Us To Our Own Devices*, the shortest song on the album. By far.

Their musical heritage derived from the 'Canterbury' sound of the late 1960's and 1970's as practised by bands such as Caravan who were, themselves, no strangers to lengthy songs. The band was the very epitome of an acquired taste, but Michael had acquired that taste and to Judy that was all that mattered. She had spent over thirty years pleasing Michael and she saw no good reason to change things now. In fact, she had a surprise planned for him tonight that should, if she knew her man, which of course she did, would please him very much.

Stefan and Jake were looking fresh after their mini drinking and mini bonding session. Michael rather less so. He had never really got the hang of alcohol consumption though he still manfully tried to keep up with everyone around him. To no avail. Judy's considered opinion garnered through the years was that Michael was a true lightweight. No one would argue the point.

Lyme's finest catering company The Fossilites had been busy laying out their wares on the tables that Judy and the girls had decorated earlier. The menu was on an Asian theme. No one knew why. There were spring rolls with a chilli dipping sauce, vegetable samosas with a yogurt and mint dip, prawns in filo pastry with a garlic and herb dip, chicken satay with peanut sauce, oriental sesame prawns on toast, filo tartlets with bang bang chicken, aromatic duck pancakes with Hoi-Sin Sauce with spring onion and cucumber, salmon teriyaki skewers with ginger and soy dip…and…well you get the idea. In an emergency for non-Asian food lovers The Fossilites would provide sausage rolls and crisps, but no pork scratchings; the company had a certain reputation to live up to.

Several guests asked Michael about the band. Was it music they could dance to? And from those who lived nearby and had heard the sound checks, was it music at all? He did have an ally; Andy Burton, who revelled in the prog-rock of the seventies onwards. Indeed, it was he who had recommended that Michael investigate Canterbury Tales, starting with their first album, *The Moon May Be Bright But Can It Ever Be Right?*, recorded in a lock-up in Walthamstow. Primitive it may have been, but it had a raw power that intrigued Michael, but very few others. The changes in personnel over the years had not in any way affected the band's vision or grandiose motifs. Robin Latimer was the fourth lead guitarist to grace the band and Michael was fervently hoping he would live up to the playing of his illustrious predecessors.

"Happy Birthday," offered Andy. "Excited about seeing the band?"

"Thanks mate and yes I am. What can you tell me about this Latimer guy?"

"Ah yes, did you get to listen to any of the Camel stuff I gave you?"

"I did yes, loved it."

"Well you remember the name of their guitarist do you?"

"Yes, Andrew Latimer. Got it, Robin is related to him."

"No."

"Inspired by him?"

"Not that I am aware of."

"Then why are you telling me this?"

"Er…I don't know."

Michael mingled, not that he ever found mingling easy. He was always wary and slightly uneasy about being the centre of attention. He had never formulated a cast-iron approach to dealing with it, chiefly because it happened so rarely.

"Mike, my ill at ease hero! What do you think so far?"

"I love it, Jude. Thank you so much for all of this."

Judy smiled and kissed him, it seemed the appropriate response. She then resumed her own mingling. Michael watched her go, she was up to something, he just knew it, but what? He had no time to ponder further for Katy and Annabelle appeared and escorted him up to the bar where one of the West Country's finest ciders awaited him; the famed Pilsdon Pocket Punch. He was invited by all those present to down it in one. The mark of a true Dorset man he was told. He raised the glass to his mouth. Twenty-one minutes later it was gone. He liked to savour his drinks; it was the mark of a true Cotswolds man. He felt good about himself; twenty-one minutes was a new personal best.

The aroma of Asian food filled the theatre. The food was going down really well. The Fossilites reputation would remain intact in spite of the four requests for sausage rolls, cheese and onion crisps and a jam and Branston pickle sandwich although the validity of the last request was hotly debated. Appetites sated. Tables cleared. Band in the bar sampling local ales and ciders; this prog-rock was thirsty work and a few ciders were deemed necessary for complex asymmetrical meters and unusual time signatures. A few late comers arriving. Apologies made and accepted. The stage curtain which had been open just a few minutes ago was now closed. Something going on behind that curtain, but what?

Judy, Annabelle and Stefan joined the man of the moment.

"All right my birthday hero?"

"Oh yes. Where have Katy and Jake got to? Not seen them for a while."

"Shh now," Judy answered as the curtain opened. Ah, there they were.

Jake was standing on one side of the stage, a take-away coffee in his hand. Katy on the other side, pacing up and down, then sitting down crossing and re-crossing her legs. It was a perfectly mimed representation of someone urgently in need of the toilet after one coffee too many. Jake now began pacing, his man-bag swinging from his arm. A garbled announcement. Exaggerated mimes of listening intently from the pair. Then they ran. Towards each other, but exiting stage left and stage right. Back they came. Towards each other, a collision now unavoidable. Katy and Jake executed perfect pratfalls.

"I'm so sorry."

"No, it was my fault entirely."

"Nothing is ever a lady's fault."

"Let me buy you a coffee at least as you seem to be wearing most of yours."

"Thank you."

"But, I have to er…go somewhere first."

"I'll see you in the coffee shop at the end of the platform then."

Cue Jake/Michael sitting at table, drumming fingers, consulting watch. Restless. Impatient. Katy/Judy enters. Sigh of relief from Jake/Michael. Introductions made.

"Canford Road, really? I am in Manchuria Road."

"Yes, just a stone's throw away then, if you have a particularly strong throwing arm, which I haven't. Do you?"

"Look at me. Do you think so?"

"No, I guess not. Do you know the Bread and Roses?"

"Is it a new band?"

"No, it's…oh, you were being funny weren't you?"

"I was trying, Michael."

"You succeeded. So, the Bread and Roses, tomorrow night perhaps, seven-thirty?"

The stage darkened. One single spotlight on Jake/Michael. 'Please say yes' he intoned over and over. The stage darkened again. A single spotlight on Katy/Judy. 'I should say no' she intoned over and over.

"Yes, I'd love that, thank you."

The curtain closed. The curtain opened. A coffee table centre stage, yes, the night of the proposal. Michael had never seen anyone fall so spectacularly into a coffee table as Jake did, it was a work of art whereas his own fall was anything but. One or two other scenes and vignettes followed, including one or two passages of his life that Michael had forgotten about.

"Well?"

"I loved it, Jude. Thank you so much. Hey, thanks guys," he said as Katy and Jake appeared.

"I bet you were embarrassed as hell, Dad!"

"I was, you know me and being the centre of attention, but I really enjoyed it. What a family I have."

"You bet," confirmed Katy. Judy and Annabelle nodded. Stefan and Jake only tentatively nodded, unsure as to their status within the family.

Now it was the turn of Canterbury Tales to 'entertain'. They launched into their opening number with a great deal of gusto, raging guitar, pounding tom-toms, heavy bass and soaring mellotron coming together with a fusion of sound unheard of in the Marine Theatre. To give the ageing prog-rockers their due they were still playing with great gusto when the song came to an end eighteen minutes later. Needless to say the bar was full by that point. They played for two hours all told during which time they managed to fit in six songs (purely by trimming some of them down). Still, Michael enjoyed it, which was after all the main thing. Oh, and Andy Burton too.

Cries of speech. Sound of Michael getting to his feet. Intake of breath Swallowing hard.

"Unaccustomed as I am…no…that doesn't work does it?"

Cries of 'no'.

"Look, it's easy really. Thank you to every one of you for coming. Thank you to Canterbury Tales for their set, great wasn't it?"

Cries of 'no'.

"Thank you to my special girls Katy and Annabelle for mostly continuing to be special. Thank you to Judy for being Judy as she has always been. Thank you."

He sat down hurriedly. He stood up hurriedly.

"And thanks to Stefan and Jake for making it so easy for me to welcome them into the family. Er…that's it."

Cue smattering of applause and a spirited attempt at 'For He's a Jolly Good Fellow'. The decision was made that the tidying up could wait until the morning. It seemed like a good decision to Michael, his cider intake had well and truly exceeded his self-imposed limits and he was in need of his bed.

As they all walked home Michael asked Judy where she had got the idea of Katy and Jake performing little snippets from their life together.

"I think because so much of it is fresh in my mind. I have been jotting down all the high points and low points we have experienced. Rather like a family history told in glimpses as opposed to a true history."

"Something to pass on down through the generations to come?"

"Something like that. I may even have a few copies made. Connor will help. I have thought of a title…"

"*Days of Lyme and Roses*?"

"No."

"*Meet the Hamiltons*?"

"No. *A Twist of Lyme*."

Chapter Eighteen-The Double Event

Two years on from when it was first mooted in the kitchen of the Old House, the 'double event' was about to happen. Katy and Jake had already set up home together, having had the opportunity to buy at a knock-down price (because most folk believed it should be knocked down) a barn conversion near to Jake's home town of Bude. The barn still needed a certain amount of converting and with both Katy and Jake touring continually; often at opposite ends of the country, finding the time necessary was anything, but easy. The barn, for all that, was very definitely a home. It had become more so of late while Katy was filming in Cornwall. She was playing the part of a fisherman's wife in a new soap opera called *Kernow People*. Her role chiefly consisted of staring out to sea; it seems fisherman's wives do that a lot in Cornwall not to mention supplying their men with hearty artery-closing breakfasts. Jake was touring Cornwall and Devon in a production of *The Thirty Nine Steps*. From coast to coast he was proclaimed as the best Richard Hannay in living memory. Mind you, there hadn't been a production of the play in either county for over forty years, but an accolade is an accolade all the same.

Annabelle's latest posting was to Coventry, near enough to Throdnall for Stefan to come and see her regularly. They had yet to take the step of living together, but they had been scouting for houses in Warwickshire and had just about settled on a house in Wellesbourne. Stefan worked in logistics, specifically vehicle delivery in which he was an especially gifted controller and communicator. He had approached a company whose head office was on the airfield at Wellesbourne, long disused by any form of air-borne transport, but a thriving industrial area. Jet Logistics jumped at the chance to have Stefan Kowalski on their team, his was a name you could trust in the world of vehicle delivery even if it couldn't always be spelt correctly.

The double wedding was taking place at the Guildhall in Lyme Regis, with its splendid view of the sea and for Michael, vivid memories of raucous council meetings attended. Michael and Judy had taken the unusual step of handling the catering themselves (not any kind of snub for The Fossilites) along with a few volunteers. The store room at the house was full of boxes of wine and Prosecco, huge amounts of jam (cream teas you see) and cream in a spare fridge. At the last moment, well not quite the last, scones and cakes would be made. Judy had taken on the mantle of her mother's cake baking and was threatening to produce a lemon drizzle cake (or three) the like of which had never been seen in Dorset. Michael suddenly discovered against all the odds that he had a knack for making scones, a knack Judy was going to make full use of.

"How many?" he asked again

"Two hundred," Judy answered again.

"Two hundred?"

"Yes, two hundred."

Fortunately this part of the scone amounts dialogue did not go on long and need not detain us for long either.

"You have a lot of faith in me."

"As always my baking hero, as far as you are concerned it's the *icing* on the cake."

"Must be why I'm so *fond*ant of you."

"Ouch! I'll have to *whip* you into shape."

"Not *beat* me with it?"

"Nor even *batter* you with it."

"Not even if I *egg* you on?

"Don't need to Mike, I have the *measure* of you."

"Hmm, if you beat me this time I will be *steaming*."

"If you do I will accept it, it's just how the *cookie* crumbles after all."

"That's just *grate!*"

"I'm on a roll, you are going to *fold* and let out a blood-*curdling* scream and leave me like the cat that's got the *cream*."

"Er…damn!"

The two days leading up to the wedding(s) had been a flurry of hard work, baking, final planning and final panicking. Nothing yet had gone wrong, but no one was counting their chickens (not that they had any). Katy and Annabelle had arrived, but were lost in make-up and hair style discussions. Stefan and Jake had arrived and were both ensconced at the Royal Lion, but had not been lost in make-up and hairstyle discussions. This was to be an old-fashioned wedding for both girls with no pre-marriage mingling although that particular ship had long since sailed.

The Marine Theatre was utilised once more, which pleased Katy especially, she was so at home in that environment. Repeated visits had been made the day before, setting up tables, decorating those tables and decorating the walls, but in a subtle way. The volunteers were finishing off the essentials on the morning of the weddings; glasses, cutlery, place settings. And also the small matter of transporting Michael's lovingly baked one hundred and ninety scones. One hundred and ninety? Yes, because three were too small, two too hard and he had eaten the other five in pursuit of quality control. Oddly enough one of Judy's lemon drizzle cakes was found to have a portion or two missing. They would later prove to be the stars of the show, her mother would have been proud of her.

The morning of the wedding(s). The kitchen a whirlpool of activity. Michael was once more putting his culinary skills to the test, creating a mountain of hotly and thickly buttered toast. Judy was right to ask whether she could have toast with her butter. Neither Katy nor Annabelle professed to be nervous, but every nuance in their voices gave them away. They were hinting at how each other's dress would look for this was something only known to themselves and to their mother who had tramped around Plymouth with Katy for a day and around Leamington Spa with Annabelle for a morning, Annabelle being that bit more decisive. Truth be known she had a much better idea what she wanted from the outset; an A-line dress with an off-the-shoulder neckline, a basque waistline which her mother argued against, an argument she was never going to win. All this was complemented by a sweep train with the dress made from Charmeuse.

Katy had opted after several hours for a more traditional approach with an organza ballgown dress, with a sheer neckline, a dropped waist and a court length train. Later on that morning they both professed each other's dress to be equally beautiful. Michael and Judy both professed that their daughters were equally beautiful which was nothing less than the truth. The boys wore suits, off the peg, but selected with great care they assured everyone. And no one had any reason to doubt that for they both looked as handsome as perhaps they had ever been. And quite possibly more so than they ever would be.

Tomas, Stefan's brother had flown in from Gdansk, very excited about being best man although unsure as to what exactly what was expected of him. The only jokes he knew were Polish ones and very popular ones at that, especially in the shipyards, but maybe too Polish and earthy for this particular occasion. Jake's best man was a fellow actor, Julian Kent-Smythe who hailed from Kent and hailed also as one of the finest Laertes this side of Denmark. Both best men were sitting down with the grooms and partaking of a breakfast any Cornish fisherman's wife would have been proud to serve up to their man. Not they didn't have faith in Michael and Judy's catering skills, for they did, they were just unsure as to how much faith so they were playing safe. As tradition goes they were doing okay, condemned men and hearty breakfasts had only surfaced three times during the cereal course and only twice after the bacon and eggs had arrived. Or *obfite śniadanie skazaniec* as Tomas put it.

A landau with a matched pair of horses had been hired to collect the lads and deposit them at the Guildhall and while they stood around trying not to look too conspicuous as the tourists gawped at them, the landau would continue on to collect the Hamiltons en masse. There was a momentary panic as the horses trotted along the driveway as they sensed certain presences in the garden, those certain presences being the good captain, his men and Irish Meg. Irish Meg, of course, had never, ever been seen by any of the occupants of the houses, but horses are a different kettle of fish and Irish Meg's flaming red hair undimmed by the intervening nigh on four hundred years would have startled any horse in the vicinity. Which is of course what happened. The Mastercoachman was just as startled as the horse albeit for a different reason and the groom had to leap into action, leap being the operative word. Now, he could have planned ahead and brought a change of trousers with him, surely tumbles onto dusty driveways were part of the job? But it seemed not. He was a slight lad and Judy had just the thing for him, pair of cropped trousers in a dashing shade of lime green. He protested that it wasn't really his colour, but a trouser emergency is a trouser emergency.

While Judy was attending to this small matter Michael was attending to the small matter of the captain and his men...and woman. Assurances were given that they would retreat to what the horses would consider a safe distance and promised Michael that they would not make any sudden moves or attempt to hum the Wedding March, although they made no such promise as regards Here Come the Bride(s).

The journey to the Guildhall was both uneventful and slow punctuated by oohs and aahs from folk who seemed to be thronging the footpaths for that very reason.

The girls remarked how it made them feel special to which their parents replied with the obvious answer; you are special. Which was undoubtedly true. The Church Street traffic problems had been alleviated recently by the simple expedient of demolishing the centuries old church. Progress, it's what happens. Although it was still slow progress through the traffic lights until they arrived at the Guildhall where the lads were waiting patiently although unknown to the landau's occupants they had nipped into the Pilot Boat for a swift half to calm their nerves. Stefan and Jake helped Annabelle and Katy down and then entered the Guildhall to await the grand arrival. Judy alighted and helped Michael down. His dodgy knees had always made alighting from carriages a tortuous thing.

The catering duties were not the only shared duties of the day, for Michael was giving Katy and away and Judy doing the honours for Annabelle. A quick check of each other's make-up, Michael being excluded, and a quick check of dresses, suit, hat and tie and away they went up the stairs. The bullet-proof perspex screen so necessary for meetings of the full council had been temporarily removed and removed to a place of safety. There was a hush inside the chamber which was doubling as a register office. The wedding party took their seats at the head of the chamber. In no time at all (well, eleven minutes actually) rings had been exchanged, vows undertaken and a register signed and a smiling Mr And Mrs Mellor and an equally smiling Mr an Mrs Kowalski were beaming at all and sundry.

The official photographer, Kathleen Tully was in her element, that is, bossing people around. It was one of her skills, everyone said so. But the end results would prove to have justified the means. Lyme Regis, as usual, provided a dramatic and beautiful backdrop to the proceedings. One or two folk drifted away towards the theatre; they had heard about the scones. One or two folk were already there; they had heard about the lemon drizzle cake.

Normal order was resumed; those in the theatre were sent back out so Katy, Jake, Annabelle and Stefan could greet them officially. Once the greetings were completed then it was a rush to the tables where Michael and Judy's volunteers were distributing cream teas and bottles of Prosecco. Jake's parents had only just arrived; a lorry shedding its load of traffic cones had brought the whole of North Cornwall to a standstill. As they entered the theatre they were still arguing as to why they had not travelled the night before. Stephen Mellor holding the view that they should have done and Liz Mellor holding a contrary view in spite of the traffic cone chaos. Wine was poured, nibbles nibbled, scones scoffed and soon came the moment that Michael was both dreading and feeling excited about in equal measure; the speech.

"Distinguished guests, those of dubious distinction and those of no distinction, family, relatives, in-laws and outlaws, young and old, friends, friends of friends, freeloaders and hangers-on, good afternoon. For those of you that don't know me, my name is Michael and I am the very proud father of these beautiful brides. For those that do know me, I am still Michael. Ladies and gentlemen, I should probably make you aware from the very start that I lack any real practical experience as a speaker. Having spent many years of my life living in a house with three women there have been few opportunities when I have been allowed to speak and even fewer opportunities when anyone has actually been listening. It may be early for the first toast, but may I propose a toast to absent friends; Stefan's parents who are unable to be with us for reasons I cannot possibly divulge. And to those who didn't live to see this day, but would have made such a difference to the day by their presence. And to Fay, Judy's sister wherever she is. Cheers! Katy and Annabelle, don't they look beautiful, such beautiful young women? I said, don't they look beautiful?"

Cries of 'yes' from the floor.

"That's better. It doesn't seem that long ago to me that they were crawling around on their hands and knees, having tantrums and vomiting all over the place…just typical teenagers really. So you can probably see that I am just so glad to give them away at last. However, I have never found giving things away easy, take a look in my wardrobe if you don't believe me and today is no exception. I know, however, that I am placing my daughters into the more than capable hands of two fine, no, very fine young men. And I would like to say at this stage; welcome to family, Stefan and Jake. Now, I know Katy and Annabelle were very keen for me not to embarrass them in any way, apart from my dancing later that is, so in deference to their wishes I have had to scrap ninety percent of my speech so at least you can be assured of one thing; it will be short. In fact it's nearly over. However, there is one person I haven't mentioned, actually there lots of people I haven't mentioned, but moving on…shall we have another toast? I said, shall we have another toast?"

Cries of 'yes' from the floor.

"That's better. To Judy, my rock, my beautiful woman who has been everything to me for so long. I see her beauty reflected in the radiant faces of Katy and Annabelle today. To Judy. Once more, I would like to welcome not just Stefan and Jake, but Stephen and Liz and young Tomas who did so well today, into our family. Welcome, all of you. And finally, echoing what you are all thinking…and finally, raise your glasses to the happy couples, Katy and Jake, Annabelle and Stefan! Oh and be careful with the table decorations, I can take them back to Poundland for a refund on Monday. Over to you, Julian."

112

Julian got to his feet and promptly sent a champagne flute crashing to the floor. His first words were therefore unrehearsed and unplanned, but simple enough. "Has anyone a dustpan and brush please?"

Someone had.

"Thank you, Michael. Ladies and gentlemen, if there's anybody here this afternoon who's feeling nervous, apprehensive and queasy at the thought of what lies ahead…… it's probably because you have just married Jake Mellor. Joking, Katy…honestly! I am glad Jake asked me to be his best man for it gives me the chance to speak for five minutes without him interrupting me. He scrubs up well doesn't he, but why he chose to copy my outfit I'll never know! You may be wondering what Katy sees in Jake. I have known him ten years and I am wondering that too. Honestly though, this is a very special privilege for me on this very emotional day. If you don't think it's emotional…look at the cake, it's in tiers. Unfortunately for the purposes of this speech Jake has lived a blameless life entirely free of embarrassing moments. Drunken nights have never played a part in his life, if they had and he happened to be in Ipswich at the time he could have ended up with a traffic cone on his head, singing 'Where did you get that hat?' outside the police station. Or…if they had and he happened to be in Llanelli at the time, he could have ended up diving naked into what he thought was the local river, but was actually the railway line. But, like I say, nights like that have never played a part. Still time I guess. Jake is making a name for himself as an actor and rightly so, he has Katy fooled after all. Seriously, it's my great pleasure to be his friend and my great privilege to be his best man. Let's raise our glasses to Jake and Katy. Jake and Katy!"

Tomas realising from the smiles and laughter that Julian's speech had been really rather good even though he had understood so little of it, was now doubly nervous. There was only one approach to his speech; it would have to be in Polish and he would rely on his brother to translate. It wasn't all in Polish admittedly; the 'hello' and 'to Stefan and Annabelle' were perfectly understood by all present. It was just the bits in between that caused problems. Stefan, as surmised by his brother, did indeed translate.

"In case you are wondering and I am sure you are, Tomas said and I quote, 'Stefan is wonderful, Annabelle is wonderful, together they are wonderful.' Well, that was the gist of it anyway."

Tomas smiled, "*Dziękuję brata.*"

"Now I am on my feet, I may well stay here. First of all, thank you to my new father-in-law for his kind words. When I say new, I don't mean I have had another because I haven't and between you and me and everyone else I will be very pleased if I have never have another. Thank you to everyone who has helped to make this day special, most of you I don't even know, but without you this would not have gone so smoothly. I would like to thank my parents who as you know cannot be here for reasons I cannot possibly divulge, but they gave me the best possible start in life, even in Gdansk. I owe them a huge debt of thanks. Now, to one of the stars of the show, Annie. When I first met Annabelle, I only had eyes for someone else. Some of you may know that someone else was in fact Katy. But, I got over that very quickly. Sorry, Katy. Three days being around Annie was enough to convince me that she was the one for me. By some stroke of fortune, she felt the same way. Sorry, Jake. Ah yes, when we met. Annie also only had eyes for someone else. Some of you may know and you certainly do now, that someone else was in fact Jake. But she got over that very quickly. Sorry, Jake. I am not good at speeches to be honest and the only thing I can really think of to say is that I am so proud to be your husband, Annie and I look forward to a long and happy life with you. To Annabelle, everybody."

"My turn now," said Jake, knowing his cue as befits an actor. "Of course the biggest thank-yous of the day have to go to our respective parents and newly formed in laws. We would like to thank them for all their help and contribution in making this day everything we could have dreamed of. Thanks to Judy for all her hard work and effort that she has put in making the cakes and all the flowers and due to the number of phone calls between Judy and mum, BT would also like to say a special thank you too. I would personally like to thank Michael and Judy for bringing up such a lovely daughter and thank you both for making me feel so welcome in your family. I am an incredibly shy person, no really, but you have made it very easy for me to fit in and I hope I can be everything you want from a son-in-law and more. I would really like to thank my mum and dad, who should undoubtedly receive a medal for endurance. They have always loved and supported me through every stage of my life, even during my surly teenager stage that seemed to last well into my twenties, and which Katy may argue hasn't ended yet. So thanks mum and dad for all the love and guidance you've given, and I hope I can make you as proud of me as I am of you. Thanks to Julian for being a best friend and best man and for very nearly not telling those stories! So to my new wife, it doesn't seem five minutes since I was proposing to you on the beach, under the stars, proposing twice to you as it happens, as you made me do it again, "because it was over too fast the first time". Sounds romantic, except it wasn't on a beach, nor under the stars, but in number three dressing room at the Clacton Empire. Regardless of that, I'm so happy to be married to this beautiful, stunning, good looking and talented woman. I suppose every groom thinks his bride is the most beautiful in the world, and today that's how I feel. To Katy, ladies and gentlemen."

Judy had thrown tradition out of the window at her wedding by making a speech of her own. Was history repeating itself as Katy and Annabelle got to their feet? Not quite. Somewhere off stage, a piano could be heard. Katy and Annabelle began quietly and then got into their stride:

"Sisters, sisters

There were never such devoted sisters,

Never had to have a chaperone, no sir,

I'm there to keep my eye on her

Caring, sharing

Every little thing that we are wearing

When a certain gentleman arrived from Rome

She wore the dress, and I stayed home

All kinds of weather, we stick together

The same in the rain and sun

Two different faces, but in tight places

We think and we act as one

Those who've seen us

Know that not a thing could come between us

Many men have tried to split us up, but no one can

Lord help the mister who comes between me and my sister

And lord help the sister, who comes between me and my man."

They had not expected a standing ovation, but they got one just the same. Everyone on the top table looked at them with varying degrees of pride, awe, bemusement and astonishment. With good reason.

"We've been practising," explained Annabelle to her tearful mother. "And Katy gave me a few pointers."

"More than a few!" added Katy.

Tables cleared. Cakes cut. More scones scoffed. Bar doing well. Much mingling. Much merriment.

The evening ended with dancing, not of all it motivated and spurred on by alcohol intake. Michael overcame his reticence for public displays of rhythm and made the dance floor his own. It was one of the highlights of the day. Everyone said so. All in all, it was a day to remember and all of them would.

There were other 'double events' to come; Jake and Katy's son, Jason was born the following year closely followed by Rosie, Stefan and Annabelle's daughter. Two years later, another double; Chloe and Daniel. Home for Jake, Katy and family was to remain the converted barn in North Cornwall which wore its agricultural past on its sleeve or more literally on its drive where a bright yellow combine harvester greeted visitors along with various implements whose usage was to remain unknown. Visitors were encouraged to give their best shots at guessing how these implements would have been used and a box was provided in the kitchen where such guesses could be dropped. The practice was discontinued when the content of some of these estimates was found to be a tad unsavoury.

Stefan, Annabelle and family continued to live in Warwickshire although the house in Wellesbourne had been considered too small and not quite rural enough so they decamped to a period cottage in the village of Warmington where the children spent many happy hours feeding the ducks in the pond on the village green and Stefan and Annabelle spent many happy hours in the Plough Inn.

There were frequent visits to Lyme and the children as they grew older were let into the 'secret' of the garden. They were rather disappointed at the hazy figures who materialised from time to time. It was not, in their view, a proper haunting at all. But they loved the sea, the beaches and the town itself.

On those occasions the family home was a proper family home once more, ringing with laughter. And there, Michael and Judy stayed. And stayed…

Chapter Nineteen-Later (A Snippet)

"The best thing we ever did," said Judy one evening, as they sipped the obligatory (still) wine in the garden, "was to move to Lyme Regis."

Michael smiled.

"The best thing I ever did of course," added Judy, "was to meet and marry you.

"I was going to say exactly that."

"What? That the best thing I ever did was to meet and marry you?"

"Yes, you know how I always agree with you, especially when you are right."

"That day at Clapham Junction station. I often think about it. What if I hadn't had three cups of coffee? What if you weren't running late? But then you were always running late weren't you. You are my tardy hero and I adore you."

He kissed her. After all these years, it was still the appropriate response. It had never been anything, but the appropriate response to tell the truth.

Chapter Twenty-Much, Much Later (AKA The End)

How lonely we shall be!

What shall we do

You without me,

I without you?

-Harold Monro, *Midnight Lamentations*

Perhaps the mark of a man, given the chance, is how he dies. For Michael, it was reasonably simple; he did not want to be a burden to Judy, he did not want her have to do everything for him. Although apart from bouts of culinary genius and washing-up perhaps it was ever thus. Michael definitely did not find dying easy; it was proving to be as complicated as life had occasionally been for him. He had throughout his life exhibited a tendency to put himself down. In truth, there were many things he actually had found easy, although they were overshadowed by the many things he did not.

He had found loving Judy extraordinarily easy. Whenever he looked back, which was often now as the future was now denied to him, he convinced himself that he had loved Judy from the very first moment they met, from the moment they crashed to the station platform together. Perhaps it could be counted as their very first public declaration of love in front of commuters who apparently took tumbles on the platform and declarations of love in their stride. Oh look, someone has fallen...look the other way, don't get involved. Oh look, someone has fallen in love...oh well, here comes the train.

He found loving Katy and Annabelle extraordinarily easy. It was true that he had not always found being a father easy, but he was hardly alone in that. There was no manual he could refer to, but the joy of fatherhood was in its unpredictability, the never knowing what was around the corner. He was proud of their achievements and he was always quick to tell them so. He had not found relinquishing them into care of others easy, but Stefan and Jake were devoted to them, whatever doubts he may have had regarding them had long since vanished. As to his own achievements, well, he was a modest man. With good reason.

And the grandchildren, those lovely grandchildren. Jason, (Judy often shuddered when she heard the name, but less so since he had been living with them), Chloe, Rosie and Daniel. All of them delightful, all of them easy to love, all of them growing up fast. He was sure whatever they did in life they would make a success of-it was in their genes although he was not sure whether they stemmed from him or Judy. He would have liked to have had more time with them, if he could do so from will-power alone then he would, but his body was not his to command now, but for all that he was satisfied even content with his life's work, his life's loves and his life's legacy.

"Hello, my hero, how are you doing today?"

"Judy, where did you appear from?"

"Probably from this chair I have been sitting in most of the night."

Michael struggled to sit up. Judy gently, very gently, pushed him back down.

"Lay still, Mike. Rest."

"That's all I can do. Rest and wait."

He closed his eyes and turned his head away. His breathing was shallow, but steady.

Judy loved her man, always had. She sometimes thought she had fallen in love with him at the very moment he ran straight into her that morning at Clapham Station. Perhaps she had, she was always more romantic than Michael although he did have his moments, many of them in fact. He had been her best friend, best lover and the finest father she had ever encountered. The finest man she had ever encountered. She knew that she would never be able to live without him, she would lose too much of herself with his passing. The future was for Katy and Annabelle and their children. Not for her, she had no need of it any more.

Arrangements had been made because they had to be. Permission had been granted for a garden burial, a humanist funeral. Michael may have briefly considered moving away from the Old House at one point, but he, like Judy, had no wish ever to leave. This step would grant them their wish.

There was a silence throughout the house that the house had never known. It had always been a busy house, a house of laughter, a house of love, a house of levity and another word beginning with L that I cannot quite bring to mind. But now Michael had awoken once more he was struck by this silence, the patient silence. The waiting silence. His lack of punctuality was well known to his family. He had never developed the knack of arriving anywhere on time. 'You'll be late for your own funeral' he had been told often. Now, he doubted this. In the gloom of the room he could see Judy, Katy and Annabelle. He smiled and slept once more.

"Comfortable?"

He opened his eyes. "Yes, Jude, comfortable. Thank you…thank you."

"No, *thank you*."

She kissed him. The appropriate response, but he was beyond feeling it.

"Goodbye, Michael my hero. I love you."

The day of the funeral was grey and overcast. The sea mist and inland fog had decided to congregate over the garden. The drizzle it produced penetrated all the raincoats and hooded jackets on show. No one minded. They were there to say their goodbyes and their thank-yous. It could have been a heat-wave with attendant warnings from the Daily Express not to venture out unless you were a mad dog or an Englishman. It could have been a blizzard with snow so deep it brought branches crashing down under the weight of the collected snow. It wouldn't have mattered.

The operator of the mechanical digger, Andrew Peters, was standing by. He was convinced that earlier when he dug out sufficient soil for the coffin he had spotted other bones in the earth. He decided that this information was best kept to himself. Let sleeping bones lie.

A few words were spoken, some irreverent because Michael would have wanted some humour injected into the proceedings. It's how he had lived his life. Everyone said so. For the most part though it was a sombre, silent affair where so many, perhaps too many memories were kept locked up. When both the rain and the occasion had reached saturation point, Andrew Peters was given the nod.

Katy nudged Annabelle.

"Look, down by the stream, that hazy figure. Is that the captain?"

It was.

In essence Judy stopped living the day Michael died. In reality she hung on for another two weeks. She, as always, had been right…living without Michael was impossible. Whatever the death certificate showed no one was in any doubt that she had died of a broken heart. She had loved Michael with all of that heart. This was possibly her greatest declaration of love for her man; rushing to be re-united with him.

The house seemed to exhale with Judy's passing. Some undefinable thing had left, perhaps the spirit of those who loved it. The house was in mourning. The day of the funeral proved to be even murkier than when Michael was laid to rest. Indeed, if you put your hands in front of your face no one would have known. A few words were spoken, many of them irreverent once more. Judy had insisted on humour and everyone valiantly rose to the occasion. Anyone passing by on that grey, dreary day would have heard laughter. Muted laughter, but laughter all same. It's how Judy wanted to go, how she hoped to go.

Andrew Peters was again doing the honours and once more he was standing respectfully by. When the cold, the wet and the occasion reached saturation point he was given the nod once more. Stefan, Jake, Jason, Chloe, Rosie and Daniel turned back towards the house. Katy and Annabelle remained a few moments longer. During those few moments, Katy nudged Annabelle.

"Look, down by the stream, those two hazy figures. Is it the captain and Irish Meg?"

It wasn't.

Epilogue

The old house was to become Jason's new house and when his children announced one summer evening many years later that they had seen Great-Granddad and Great-Grandma in the garden he was not in the least surprised. Their imprint and spirit filled the house.

Everyone said so.

Acknowledgements and notes.

Now, I may have said this before, but this really is the end of the Hamilton saga. There will be no Christmas specials, no reunions, nothing, it's all over. But, I have enjoyed their fellowship very much and it has been fun. Well, for me anyway. The measures taken to curb tourism in Lyme Regis are entirely fictitious and with any luck will remain so. You will look in vain for Throdnall in your atlases, it does not exist. But everywhere else mentioned does. Even Banbury. Continuing thanks to all who are supportive of me and occasionally say nice things about what I produce. Continuing thanks to Gill, who as always, tries to keep me on the grammatical straight and narrow. If I stray from that path sometimes then the error lies with me and me alone. I should say here that one chapter is almost entirely Gill's work. Thanks to Hannah Tarrant for suggesting the character of Hannah Tarrant! They only thing they have in common however is a fondness for chicken nuggets.

Thank you once more to Steve@MX Publishing and Bob@Staunch for giving life to this book.

And now a bonus: *Sherlock Holmes and the Scarborough Affair* is due to be published in 2015. This is a collaboration with former Bridport Prize winner, Gill Stammers[2], although to be perfectly honest my input is fairly minimal. I suppose I am more of a consultant than co-writer. But yes, the bonus. Turn the page to discover the opening chapter of *Sherlock Holmes and the Scarborough Affair…*

---

[2] Gill has asked me to point out that when she won in 1977 it was a local competition not the international one it has now grown into.

Sherlock Holmes

And The

Scarborough Affair

~

Gill Stammers and David Ruffle

Chapter One

I find recorded in my notebook that it was the summer of 1901and it was one of those almost unbearably hot days that Londoners seem to be both destined and determined to suffer in silence and with stoicism that natives of some European cities would find somewhat incomprehensible. The sunlight poured like honey off the tall, tightly-packed buildings and swept down to the over-crowded pavements below. The sun's rays bounced off the windows of the city and radiated throughout the busy thoroughfares; the heat ricocheting and magnifying its way through this great metropolis.

The heat of the day was no less noticeable in our Baker Street sitting-room and the open windows failed in any meaningful way to alleviate or negate the uncomfortable conditions. Sherlock Holmes, however, was not affected to any great degree by these hot-house conditions; he was bent over his chemistry table, intent on his experiments as he had been for the better part of the morning.

Although my experiences in India and Afghanistan had to some extent made me accustomed to the heat, I was in desperate need of fresh, albeit warm air. Not that I was particularly in need of exercise, I had only just recovered from my exertions on the continent on the trail of the vanished Lady Frances Carfax; I was fortunate in that Lausanne displayed none of the heat that we in England had been subjected to of late. Although it had been a barren year for Holmes by way of remarkable cases, the cases that we had been involved in seemed to require more physical exertions on my part than I had become accustomed to. In May we were called on to look into the abduction of Lord Saltire, the son and heir of the Duke of Holdernesse, a case which ended successfully with the safe return of son to father although there were certain aspects of the resolution of the affair that caused me some disquiet, although this is perhaps not the place to air that disquiet. This investigation required a certain amount of traversing the moors of the Peak District, 'uphill and down dale' is the phrase which most readily springs to mind.

When, added to this were the various trips to Lyme Regis to see my intended, Mrs Beatrice Heidler, including the splendid occasion of her son Nathaniel's marriage to Miss Elizabeth Hill, then I felt perfectly justified in feeling somewhat jaded. Beatrice was going to be away throughout the latter part of August and the early part of September, visiting a cousin in Margate whose confinement was fast approaching. In the meantime, Nathaniel would take over the running of his mother's boarding house ably assisted by young Lydia, but knowing Lydia as I did, I suspected it was Nathaniel who would be doing the assisting. I knew I would be a distraction or worse to Beatrice were I to inflict Margate with my presence, but I felt the need to get away from the city for a while if my dwindling funds would allow such a course of action.

"I am going for a stroll to Hyde Park, Holmes, would you care to accompany me or do you prefer to be shut up here with your chemicals and test tubes containing God knows what?"

"You go if you wish, Watson. I am content to remain here. This particular experiment is at a crucial juncture and the delights of Hyde Park do not hold a candle to the outcome of this test, assuming I am right in my hypothesis."

"Very well, Holmes. I will see you a little later."

I returned some two hours later, no less warm, but certainly rejuvenated, to find Holmes stretched out on the chaise-longue, his eyes closed and looking for the world as if he were asleep. His eyes flicked open as I approached him.

"Sorry to disappoint you, Watson, I am not so enfeebled yet as to require an afternoon nap."

"It would be of no consequence to me whatsoever, Holmes, I assure you." I said, as I seated myself.

"I sense an eagerness to remove yourself from the city, am I correct?"

"I could say when are you not, my dear fellow? But, yes, I do feel in need of a break to recharge my batteries. Do you not feel the need yourself, Holmes?"

"Work is the best antidote to everything and my work is my life, I have no need to be rejuvenated by days by the sea or in the countryside when the cases that come my way serve that very purpose for me. And my friend, remember, my last two experiences of life by the sea were in Lyme Regis and you know full well what happened on those occasions."

"I hardly need to tell you of all people, that crime can occur anywhere and the fact that we encountered such evil in Lyme Regis hardly negates the fact that Lyme and many other resorts have much to recommend them to the flagging spirits of jaded souls."

"To me, the notion of taking the sea air for one's health is a foreign one. The effect must perforce be temporary and all too soon those that proclaim and trumpet the merits of such remedies are thrown back into their commonplace existence. My little problems help me to escape that commonplace of existence."

"Is not that effect temporary too?"

"No, because one is followed by another; a never-ending chain of conundrums and puzzles," he answered

"If that were true, Holmes, you would never have had the need for artificial stimulants."

"In order not to offend your sensibilities, perhaps I should say it is generally true. Perhaps the letter which arrived this morning while you were out will provide an opportunity for your escape from the metropolis," Holmes said, waving a bony hand towards the table.

I picked up the envelope which bore both a House of Commons imprint and a Surrey postmark. As I slid out the contents, some tickets fell out onto the carpet. On picking them up I was much surprised to see they were passes to every day's play at the Scarborough Cricket Festival. An explanation for those unfamiliar with the festival is called for; The Scarborough Festival is an end of season series of cricket matches featuring Yorkshire County cricket club, which has been held in Scarborough, on the east coast of Yorkshire, since1876. The ground, at North Marine Road, sees large crowds of holiday makers watching a mixture of first class county cricket, one day fixtures and invitation XIs in the early September sunshine every year. Many of the world's greatest cricketers have played in festival matches in recent years.

In the envelope was a covering letter from the Hon. William Thomson. His name was immediately familiar to me, not only because he was a rising star in Lord Salisbury's government, but also as a cricketer of some note. A former Oxford University cricketer who now plays his cricket for Surrey, when his tenure in the government allows him the time to do so. There was yet another reason for the familiarity of the name for we had met some months previously in rather bizarre circumstances.

****

Our paths had crossed earlier in the year when he and his wife were thrown from a hansom cab whose driver inexpertly negotiated the corner of Tottenham Court Road and Oxford Street, colliding with a furniture van. It was the time of the heaviest congestion and I had observed the accident as I was making my way towards the junction. The incident caused a good deal of chaos and whilst a number of people became involved in attempting to disentangle the frightened horses, I observed a lady lying immobile and seemingly unnoticed, in grave danger of being trampled by the horse of the furniture van, who, once freed, attempted to take flight. I instinctively pushed my way forward through the melee and whilst protecting her from the horse, gently pulled her to safety. As I was examining her for injuries, a dazed figure approached. Although bleeding profusely from a head wound, the man's only concern was for the lady's condition. It was evident that he was her husband and I allowed him to kneel beside her and take her hand while I examined her.

With necessary brevity, I informed the man that I was a doctor and returning my full attention to his wife, ascertained that she was suffering from concussion and a fractured leg. My action in pulling her from the area of danger may have exacerbated the seriousness of the fracture, but instinct and medical training told me that this had been the only course of action open to me in order to prevent far greater or even a fatal injury.

My immediate concern was to immobilise the broken leg and to that end I set about fashioning a splint from an advertising hoarding which had also been a casualty of the accident. I instructed the man to assist, requesting he remove his braces in order to bind the splint with them.

As we were completing this task, the lady was just recovering consciousness and was clearly in great distress. At this point, I was relieved to hear the clanging of the ambulance bell. I suggested to the man that he allow me to examine his head wound while his wife was lifted gently onto a stretcher. Instead of which, he took me by surprise by grasping my hand and thanking me profusely. I just had time to hand him my card with the utterance of further help, if required, dying on my lips as the injured man sprinted up the road after the ambulance. Any concern for his well-being was tempered by the fact that Barts was only a few minutes' away and he would receive any necessary treatment there.

I was approached by one of the constables, a PC Hackett, attending the scene and gave him a full account of what I had witnessed. I continued my way home, going over the events in my mind. The injured lady's husband was vaguely familiar, but I could not place him. On my return home, I was in time for afternoon tea. I felt it extraordinary that life, such as it was, at 221b Baker Street was continuing in the usual ritualistic way and yet a young lady almost lost her life during a brief interlude. It does not, however, do, to dwell on the fact that life and death is played out daily on our streets.

I regaled Holmes with the events of the afternoon, simple relief at the lady's survival causing me to play down my actions. Although giving only the bare bones of the story, his look of extreme languor and indifference silenced me before I could muse further on the identity of the couple.

The following morning, I found Holmes already partaking of his breakfast. He glanced in my direction and then without a word returned his attention to his ham and eggs, however, not before I had caught a mischievous look in his eye.

"Another mystery solved and before breakfast at that," Holmes said, laughing in his peculiar silent fashion.

Before I could question this puzzling statement, Holmes slid the morning paper across the table to me. It was evident that he had already read it as its condition was a crumpled mass. Each morning it was my fervent hope that I would get to the newspaper before Holmes. Although I could have my own copy delivered, I succeeded more often than not owing generally to Holmes's irregularity of routine. The small triumph I felt on beating him to it far outweighed the occasional effort required to straighten each and every page.

I was taken by surprise to see my name beneath the headline on the leading story.

"Quite the hero it seems, Watson," said Holmes, his voice full of amusement.

I ignored him and smoothing out the page on the table, proceeded to read the story in full, exercising my right to silence before responding to Holmes's charge.

I had no need to muse further on the identity of the couple involved in the previous day's accident. The newspaper carried a full account of the incident and informed me that the unfortunate couple was the Conservative Member of Parliament, the Honourable William Thomson and his wife, Miranda. The report went on to greatly exaggerate my part in the episode.

"Hardly a hero, Holmes. The newspaper correspondent has embellished somewhat on the simple fact that a lady was in need of medical attention and I happened to be on hand."

"It is not a fact, then, that you pulled Mrs Thomson from the hooves of a startled horse?"

"It is a fact that I removed her to a position of safety in order to attend to her injuries. Anyone would have done the same under the circumstances, you included, Holmes."

"Modesty becomes you, Watson, however, a hero you are, in the eyes of the press and not least in those of the Thomson's.

****

As I examined the tickets, I felt a flush of pleasure, but my mind immediately began to ponder the practicalities of travel to and accommodation in this most fashionable of resorts. Lodgings would be at a premium for the duration of the festival.

"Perhaps you should read the letter, Watson, before despondency descends upon you," said Holmes, breaking in on my thoughts as he is wont to do.

"Thank you Holmes, I was just about to do so," I replied with some asperity.

The content of the letter dispelled my uncertainties instantaneously. My association with Mr Thomson since his wife's accident and fortunately, expedient recovery, had been occasional. I visited Mrs Thomson soon after her admittance to hospital and once or twice during her recuperation at home. The Thomsons had their own physician, a Dr John Routley, but I felt a sense of duty regarding the fractured leg and gained great peace of mind from learning that the fracture had been clean and not aggravated by moving the casualty. On these visits Mr Thomson greeted me with the utmost cordiality and warmth; however, I hardly expected such a gift as this. Not only had he presented me with passes for the Scarborough Festival, but had also reserved accommodation for me, at his expense, at the Grand Hotel, known to be one of the finest establishments in Europe.

"I see that I was right, Watson; you have your escape."

I turned to Holmes, eyebrows raised.

"It is quite simple," he chuckled, "the deduction was ridiculously easy and as always your features gave you away. The letter bears the imprint of the House of Commons; therefore, the most likely source was the Conservative member for Guildford, with whom you have a connection, not only professionally, but personally inasmuch as you saved the life of his wife. Do not protest the fact, my friend. Even with my limited knowledge of the sporting world, I am aware that William Thomson plays a major role in the organisation of the Scarborough Festival. I have no doubt that during your visits to check on Mrs Thomson's welfare, you and her husband would have been unable to resist discussion regarding your mutual passion, puzzling though it may be to me. On seeing tickets flutter to the floor, what other conclusion could I come to other than the obvious one that they allow free passage to the festival? Further evidence came on your countenance. First, evident delight, followed by despondency as you sought to reconcile the desire to attend, with your straitened finances. As you read the letter, the sudden look of rapture suggested an unexpected and substantial bonus. It has clearly removed all your concerns, therefore, I suggest that not only has accommodation been provided for you, but further, I believe Mr Thomson holds you in such esteem that only the Grand Hotel at Scarborough will suffice."

"Correct in every detail, you really are a marvel."

Holmes sank back in his chair with a self-satisfied smile on his face. He was always warmed by genuine admiration; the characteristic of the real artist. He was also accessible upon the side of flattery and for Holmes at least it seemed difficult to differentiate one from the other!

Choosing to no longer massage Holmes's ego, I busied myself examining the passes. It was only then that I realised they were for two people, a fact that I related to Holmes.

Holmes cut me short.

"The very thought of day after day of unending idleness in the watching of a sport that moves at a snail's pace followed by dinner, each evening, dressed up to the nines in frock coat and bow tie is frankly unendurable."

"You protest too much!" I declared indignantly.

137

"You offend too easily," Holmes replied with equanimity.

"I stand by my words as I recall your obvious delight when watching Victor Trumper bat his way to a triple century against Sussex two years ago."

"I believe it was the science of his play; his placement of the ball and the merciful speed of his achievement that deserved merit. That one occasion has had no tempering on my feelings towards the sport."

I could not help, but smile for there by the fireside stood Victor Trumper's bat, a gift from the great batsman himself, treasured by Holmes, as the occasional smell of linseed oil bore witness to.

"If not for the cricket, then for Scarborough, the pull of the sea and air, clean and pure."

"What would you have me do, Watson, purchase a parasol and stroll gaily along the promenade?"

"It is precisely what I would prescribe, Holmes and I am sure the ladies of Scarborough would find your parasol somewhat recherché."

"It will not do, Watson. I have no need of a holiday, particularly the kind that you would have in store for me in Scarborough. Besides, I have two cases coming to maturity; that of the peculiar persecution of Professor Pullinger and the minor yet intriguing matter of the scandal surrounding the music-hall act, Quigley and Miller in regard to their appearance at the Tattershall Club in Carr Street."

I argued no further; the matter was closed and as far as I was aware was likely to remain so. Fate, however had other plans.

Also from David Ruffle

Sherlock Holmes and The Lyme Regis Horror, and the sequels
Sherlock Holmes and The Lyme Regis Legacy and Sherlock
Holmes and The Lyme Regis Trials

Sherlock Holmes – Tales from the Stranger's Room
(Vol 1 and 2)
An eclectic collection of writings from twenty Holmes writers.

Also from David Ruffle

Sherlock Holmes and The Missing Snowman

A young girl's snowman has gone missing. Where can it have gone? There is only one man who can help. Sherlock Holmes, the most famous detective in the world.

www.mxpublishing.com

Also from MX Publishing

MX Publishing is the world's largest specialist Sherlock Holmes publisher, with over a hundred titles and fifty authors creating the latest in Sherlock Holmes fiction and non-fiction.

From traditional short stories and novels to travel guides and quiz books, MX Publishing cater for all Holmes fans.

The collection includes leading titles such as *Benedict Cumberbatch In Transition* and *The Norwood Author* which won the 2011 Howlett Award (Sherlock Holmes Book of the Year).

MX Publishing also has one of the largest communities of Holmes fans on Facebook with regular contributions from dozens of authors.

www.mxpublishing.com

Also from MX Publishing

Sherlock Holmes Short Story Collections

Sherlock Holmes and the Murder at the Savoy

Sherlock Holmes and the Skull of Kohada Koheiji

Look out for the new novel from Mike Hogan
– *The Scottish Question.*

www.mxpublishing.com

Also from MX Publishing

Our bestselling books are our short story collections;

'Lost Stories of Sherlock Holmes' , 'The Outstanding Mysteries of
Sherlock Holmes', The Papers of Sherlock Holmes Volume 1 and
2, 'Untold Adventures of Sherlock Holmes' (and the sequel
'Studies in Legacy) and 'Sherlock Holmes in Pursuit', 'The
Cotswold Werewolf and Other Stories of Sherlock Holmes' – and
many more……

www.mxpublishing.com

Also from MX Publishing

"Phil Growick's, 'The Secret Journal of Dr Watson', is an adventure which takes place in the latter part of Holmes and Watson's lives. They are entrusted by HM Government (although not officially) and the King no less to undertake a rescue mission to save the Romanovs, Russia's Royal family from a grisly end at the hand of the Bolsheviks. There is a wealth of detail in the story but not so much as would detract us from the enjoyment of the story. Espionage, counter-espionage, the ace of spies himself, double-agents, double-crossers...all these flit across the pages in a realistic and exciting way. All the characters are extremely well-drawn and Mr Growick, most importantly, does not falter with a very good ear for Holmesian dialogue indeed. Highly recommended. A five-star effort."

The Baker Street Society

Links

MX Publishing are proud to support the Save Undershaw campaign – the campaign to save and restore Sir Arthur Conan Doyle's former home. Undershaw is where he brought Sherlock Holmes back to life, and should be preserved for future generations of Holmes fans.

SaveUndershaw

www.saveundershaw.com

Sherlockology

www.sherlockology.com

MX Publishing

www.mxpublishing.com

You can read more about Sir Arthur Conan Doyle and Undershaw in Alistair Duncan's book (share of royalties to the Undershaw Preservation Trust) – *An Entirely New Country* and in the amazing compilations *Sherlock's Home – The Empty House* and the new book *Two, To One, Be* (all royalties to the Trust).